Y0-CDD-367

COMMAND PERFORMANCE

The night was dark—dark enough to keep the Cheyenne from finding them until the dawn. But the stars were out now—and by their light Ruff could see Jan Clark. Her glasses were off and her white blouse was wet, clinging to her breasts.

"Cold," she said. "I'm cold, Mr. Justice, and wet, and we might die up here."

"We won't die," Ruff said.

"No? You guarantee that?" Jan Clark smiled faintly.

Her hand took his and placed it over her breast. Her heart was thudding like a hammer.

"Show me everything, Justice," she said. "This might be my last night."

That might be true, Ruff Justice thought, but he'd do his damnedest to make it her best. . . .

⊘ SIGNET　　　　　　　　　　　　　　　　　　(0451)

Wild Westerns by Warren T. Longtree

☐	RUFF JUSTICE #1: SUDDEN THUNDER	(126599—$2.50)
☐	RUFF JUSTICE #2: NIGHT OF THE APACHE	(110293—$2.50)
☐	RUFF JUSTICE #4: WIDOW CREEK	(114221—$2.50)
☐	RUFF JUSTICE #5: VALLEY OF GOLDEN TOMBS	(115635—$2.50)
☐	RUFF JUSTICE #6: THE SPIRIT WOMAN WAR	(117832—$2.50)
☐	RUFF JUSTICE #7: DARK ANGEL RIDING	(118820—$2.50)
☐	RUFF JUSTICE #8: THE DEATH OF IRON HORSE	(121449—$2.50)
☐	RUFF JUSTICE #9: WINDWOLF	(122828—$2.50)
☐	RUFF JUSTICE #10: SHOSHONE RUN	(123883—$2.50)
☐	RUFF JUSTICE #11: COMANCHE PEAK	(124901—$2.50)
☐	RUFF JUSTICE #12: PETTICOAT EXPRESS	(127765—$2.50)
☐	RUFF JUSTICE #13: POWER LODE	(128788—$2.50)
☐	RUFF JUSTICE #14: THE STONE WARRIORS	(129733—$2.50)
☐	RUFF JUSTICE #15: CHEYENNE MOON	(131177—$2.50)
☐	RUFF JUSTICE #16: HIGH VENGEANCE	(132009—$2.50)
☐	RUFF JUSTICE #17: DRUM ROLL	(132815—$2.50)
☐	RUFF JUSTICE #18: THE RIVERBOAT QUEEN	(134125—$2.50)
☐	RUFF JUSTICE #19: FRENCHMAN'S PASS	(135288—$2.50)
☐	RUFF JUSTICE #20: THE SONORA BADMAN	(136233—$2.75)
☐	RUFF JUSTICE #21: THE DENVER DUCHESS	(137752—$2.75)
☐	RUFF JUSTICE #22: THE OPIUM QUEEN	(138635—$2.75)
☐	RUFF JUSTICE #23: THE DEATH HUNTERS	(140133—$2.75)
☐	RUFF JUSTICE #24: FLAME RIVER	(141253—$2.75)

Prices slightly higher in Canada

Buy them at your local bookstore or use this convenient coupon for ordering.

NEW AMERICAN LIBRARY,
P.O. Box 999, Bergenfield, New Jersey 07621

Please send me the books I have checked above. I am enclosing $_____
(please add $1.00 to this order to cover postage and handling). Send check
or money order—no cash or C.O.D.'s. Prices and numbers are subject to change
without notice.

Name_____

Address_____

City_____State_____Zip Code_____
Allow 4-6 weeks for delivery.
This offer is subject to withdrawal without notice.

RUFF JUSTICE #26

Twisted Arrow

by
Warren T. Longtree

Ⓢ

A SIGNET BOOK

NEW AMERICAN LIBRARY

PUBLISHER'S NOTE

This novel is a work of fiction. Names, characters, places, and incidents either are the product of the author's imagination or are used fictitiously, and any resemblance to actual persons, living or dead, events, or locales is entirely coincidental.

NAL BOOKS ARE AVAILABLE AT QUANTITY DISCOUNTS WHEN USED TO PROMOTE PRODUCTS OR SERVICES. FOR INFORMATION PLEASE WRITE TO PREMIUM MARKETING DIVISION. NEW AMERICAN LIBRARY. 1633 BROADWAY. NEW YORK. NEW YORK 10019.

Copyright © 1986 by New American Library

All rights reserved

The first chapter in this book appeared in *Jack of Diamonds*, the twenty-fifth volume of this series.

 SIGNET TRADEMARK REG. U.S. PAT. OFF. AND FOREIGN COUNTRIES
REGISTERED TRADEMARK—MARCA REGISTRADA
HECHO EN CHICAGO. U.S.A.

SIGNET, SIGNET CLASSIC, MENTOR, PLUME, MERIDIAN AND NAL BOOKS are published by New American Library,
1633 Broadway, New York, New York 10019

First Printing, June, 1986

1 2 3 4 5 6 7 8 9

PRINTED IN THE UNITED STATES OF AMERICA

RUFF JUSTICE

He knew the West better than any man alive—a hostile, savage land rife with both violent outlaws and courageous adventurers. But Ruff Justice had a sixth sense that kept him breathing and saw his enemies dead. A scout for the U.S. Cavalry, he was paid to protect the public, and nobody was faster at sniffing out a killer, a crook, a con man—red or white, at close range or far. Anyone on the wrong side of the law would have to reckon with the menace of Ruff's murderously sharp stag-handled bowie knife, with his Colt pistol, and the Spencer rifle he cradled in his arms.

Ruff Justice, gentleman and frontier philosopher—good men respected him, bad men feared him, and women, good and bad, wanted him with all the wildness of the Old West.

1

The band struck up again and the dancers moved out onto the floor. The big man with the red beard was pretty well drunk and he glowered at them. The band wasn't much, but it managed to fill Dakota Territory's Bismarck town hall with plenty of noise. Even if the tuba player did look like he was ready to expire from the effort of forcing deep notes from his huge brassy instrument.

The celebration, if it could be called that, was for the citizens of the town of Clear Creek—or rather the survivors of Clear Creek. Stone Eyes, the Cheyenne renegade, had burned the town to the ground, keeping most of its inhabitants in a state of siege for nearly a week until the army had arrived, and killing or wounding more than two dozen men and women.

Jake Troll was one of the survivors. He was big, red-bearded, and red-eyed, staggering drunk. He didn't like dances, he didn't like tuba music; he especially didn't like the fancy dude who spun by with young Jenny Farnsworth in his arms.

Jenny was smiling brightly, her eyes alight with some emotion she had never displayed to Jake Troll, though Troll had been courting her for some time now.

"What the hell's that supposed to be?" Troll grumbled to his silent companion, a one-armed, rail-thin man called Skitch.

"What?" Skitch had his own drinking to do. His head came up slowly and some sort of distant comprehension crept into his befuddled expression. "Him?" Skitch pointed to the tall man in the dark suit, string tie, ruffled shirt, and highly polished black boots. He wore his hair brushed down past his shoulders; his dark mustache drooped to his jawline. As the two men watched he threw back his head and laughed heartily.

Jenny Farnsworth placed one gloved, demure hand over her lips in a vain effort to hold back her answering laugh.

"Him," Jake Troll nodded. "What in Christ's name is he supposed to be? Ruffles and lace, for Christ's sake. That supposed to be a man?"

Skitch took a thoughtful sip of his lemonade, which had a suspicious brown hue to it. He shook his head. "Don't you remember seeing him out there, at Clear Creek?"

"I had more important things to see at Clear Creek than some dude. I had Indians to look at." Jake puffed up a little. He had killed his first man back there, an attacking Cheyenne warrior, and you'd have thought he had made the plains safe forever.

"That's that army scout, Ruff Justice," Skitch reminded his bearded friend.

Jake Troll abandoned the pretense that he was sipping the Clear Creek Ladies Club's lemonade. He swigged his whiskey from the bottle now, looking around belligerently to see if anyone had the nerve to say anything to him about it.

No one had any such intention. Jake Troll was a massive man, filled with self-importance and meanness.

8

"That's my girl," he said in a deeply slurred voice. Skitch didn't even glance at him. "Jenny Farnsworth is my girl." Still Skitch didn't answer. It was best not to say anything at all to Troll when he got in these moods.

Skitch saw the tall man who was dancing with Jenny Farnsworth smile again. Then Ruff Justice bent his head a little and whispered something into her ear. She had a pretty little, round pink ear, scrubbed and wholesome, and Skitch couldn't blame Justice for adding a little kiss to it as he drew away.

Jake Troll roared and slammed his bottle down on a nearby table, upsetting a flower arrangement the ladies had placed there. He stalked across the floor through the whirling dancers, his feet moving in time to the blasting of the tuba.

Skitch shook his head, sipped at his well-laced lemonade, and stood ready to watch the fun.

"You," Troll's voice boomed. "I want to talk to you."

Ruff Justice glanced at the big red-bearded man who stood hunched in the middle of the dance floor. Then he led the light, pretty woman in his arms past the drunk in a graceful turning dance step.

Troll tried to put a hand on Justice's shoulder, but it wasn't that easy as the couple dipped and twirled away, still smiling and talking in low voices while the band worked valiantly on.

"Was he talking to me?" Ruff Justice asked.

"Who?" They were inside the town hall, but somehow there was starlight in Jenny Farnsworth's deep-brown eyes. She held one of the tall army scout's hands in her own, while her other hand held his shoulder, lightly squeezing it from time to time.

They worked their way around the dance floor, leaving the red-bearded man to stand, bearlike, in the center of the room.

"Him," Ruff Justice said, inclining his head. "I thought he said something to me."

Jenny Farnsworth glanced that way, grimaced, and said, "Oh, that's just Jake Troll."

"Friend of yours?"

"He wants to marry me. He beats up any man who's nice to me." The girl shrugged.

"Fine," Justice said with a smile. "Jenny, you ought to tell me these things."

"It only happens when he's drunk. I didn't think he'd had time yet."

Ruff peered down into those brown eyes, wondering at her logic. But then it wasn't logic that attracted Ruff Justice to this one. The woman was young and compactly built, with an astonishing firmness of body. Jenny was full-breasted and eager to laugh, her mouth wide and sensual.

"You," a voice called from far away. This time Justice ignored him. He didn't like drunks; he especially didn't like belligerent drunks; most particularly he didn't like drunks who wanted to prove some point the day after Justice and the army had just completed a bloody, tedious, frustrating cat-and-mouse game with the elusive Stone Eyes. They'd had to drag the people of Clear Creek out of their razed town and rush them across the prairie to the safety of Bismarck.

But Jake Troll wouldn't let it go. The band staggered to a halt and Troll's voice roared out in the sudden silence.

"I'm talking to you, tall man. Dude. I want to talk to you, boy. Outside."

"Oh," Jenny Farnsworth said in frustration, "I just didn't think he'd had time yet to get plastered." Her tiny fists bunched and she smiled ingenuously at Ruff, who turned, sized up his man, and answered.

"He's had time," Justice said.

10

"Well, then, you'll have to let him beat you up. Or," she added brightly, "you could shoot him."

"I could shoot him," Ruff repeated in wonder.

"I know you have a gun. It's in your shoulder holster. Right there." She tapped the holster and the little Colt New Line .41 that rode there. Ruff's town gun.

"You!" Troll bellowed. Heads turned and people stood watching.

"Doesn't anyone ever grow up?" Justice muttered. "I'll be back," he told Jenny Farnsworth.

"Are you going to shoot him?" she asked a little too eagerly.

"Jenny, you're a darling, but I don't know about this side of you."

"In Clear Creek everyone always shot one another."

God, she was lovely. And she was very young.

"You!"

"I'll be back," Ruff said, patting her shoulder. "Save the next dance."

"Can't I watch?" Her eyes searched Ruff's and he smiled a little uneasily.

"Not this time. I'll let you watch the next time I shoot somebody."

"Oh, thank you," she said, and Ruff began to wonder about the future of this relationship.

He turned away and walked toward the hulking, red-bearded figure who stood watching him, waiting. The band struck up again as Ruff Justice reached Troll.

"Outside," Troll said with malicious glee.

"I'll miss this dance."

"You'll miss more than that."

"Oh, Mr. Justice," a heavily powdered woman of fifty called, waving a handkerchief. "When are you going to sing for us?"

Troll's lips twisted contemptuously.

"Later, Mrs. Anderson," Ruff Justice called back.

"You sing for the ladies, do you?" Troll said. They were nearly at the door.

"Works wonders. But you wouldn't understand that, friend."

Outside, the air was cool. Down the street Bismarck's saloons roared with activity. The stars were bright and close.

"You know, Troll, this is a waste of energy and time. Why don't you wander off and find yourself something else to drink?"

"Why don't you go to hell?" Troll threw a right-hand hook at Justice's head. It missed by a foot, Ruff had been anticipating the sucker punch. He pulled back his head, took Troll by his coat front, and yanked him close, driving one knee up into the big man's groin.

Troll folded up with a sickening groan and Ruff brought both interlocked hands into the red-bearded man's face. Troll tottered backward, flipped over a hitching rail, and fell on the street, to lie still and peaceful against the earth.

The scream from inside the dance hall brought Justice's head around sharply. He rushed inside as the band broke off in the middle of its number.

A crowd had gathered around something in the center of the dance floor; that something was a dead man. Ruff Justice pushed his way through.

He didn't know the man who was lying facedown on the floor, an arrow in his back. An arrow such as Justice had never seen.

It was covered with crow feathers. Instead of being straight, the shaft was twisted, as if its maker had patiently taken growing arrowweed and tied it as it grew to form the odd shape. There was no paint on the arrow.

"Where in hell did that come from?" someone asked, but there was no answer. The recent Indian fears came back and the survivors of Clear Creek glanced around nervously, some moving toward their weapons stored in the cloakroom.

"How could someone shoot Clive? God's sake, we'd have to have seen a man with a bow and arrow."

But no one had, or no one remembered having seen anything. And at first no one noticed the dully shining, nearly round object lying near the dead man's hand.

It was left to Ruff Justice to crouch and pick it up. He turned it in the lantern light and let it gleam: it was Spanish, it was ancient.

It was gold.

2

The colonel was in a sour mood. His gray eyes lifted as the tall, buckskinned scout entered his office and tossed his white stetson hat onto the hat tree in the opposite corner.

"Damn all, Justice," Col. MacEnroe said, "how in hell do you do it?"

"Practice," Ruff Justice said, looking at the hat tree.

"Not the hat! I mean this dance last night."

"Oh, that," Justice said. "Nothing to it, sir. Just put one foot in front of the other."

The commanding officer of Fort Lincoln, Dakota Territory, wasn't smiling. Justice lowered himself into a straight-backed wooden chair and steepled his fingers. MacEnroe struggled with a few unspoken caustic remarks and then asked, "What happened there last night, Ruffin?"

"It's all in the report. Everything I know, everything the marshal learned, which is damned little."

"That, I can see. Do you know who Clive Hickam was?"

"I haven't got the faintest idea," Ruff answered. "I never met him when he was alive."

"He was a scientist," MacEnroe informed his scout. "A well-respected archaeologist. The first such man to really investigate the Indian mound culture in the East, a Yale professor, an author and a lecturer."

"What was he doing living in Clear Creek?" Justice asked.

"It was only temporary." The colonel glanced at the closed office door and reached into his bottom desk drawer for his bottle of bonded bourbon. He opened the whiskey, poured himself three fingers in a gray glass, and put the bottle away. "Doctor Hickam was very interested in what he called the Alpha Cave Civilization." The colonel flipped over a sheet of blue paper. "I know this because it's written down, Justice. It doesn't mean a hell of a lot to me. All I know is that the professor had discovered, or thought he had discovered a civilization that predates the Sioux culture by a good many years—centuries, it seems."

"That's not too surprising," Justice said. "Both the Sioux and the Cheyenne lived in Minnesota, even farther north and east once upon a time. They were primarily farmers, but with the coming of the horse they moved west onto the plains. They call it the time they 'lost the corn.' "

"If there was an earlier people, nothing at all is known about them," MacEnroe went on after a sip of whiskey. "I suppose the nomadic tribes wiped them out."

"Where were they supposed to have lived?" the scout asked.

"Down along the Heart River, near Twin Buttes, according to Hickam."

"I've never seen anything down that way that looked like an old Indian site, but then I suppose Hickam was better trained in knowing what to look for."

"Maybe it was all his imagination, I wouldn't know," the colonel responded.

"Maybe." Justice's expression grew distant.

The colonel prodded him. "What is it, Ruff?"

"Nothing much. Did you see the arrow that killed Hickam?"

"I saw it. What in hell *was* that? I've never seen anything made that way. Not with crow feathers like that."

"Neither have I."

The colonel finished his drink and looked at Justice thoughtfully, turning the glass in his hands. "You're not telling me some member of an ancient tribe made that arrow, are you, Ruff?"

"I'm not telling you anything, sir."

Now the colonel seemed to be indulged in distant thoughts. Sunlight beamed through the high, narrow window of his office and painted a wedge of yellow on the plank floor. "A member of a vanished tribe who wanted revenge for Hickam's having dug up a burial site, perhaps?" The colonel smiled at his own suggestion.

"Have you ever considered writing dime novels?" Justice asked, and the colonel's smile broadened.

"Who killed Hickam?"

"No idea," Justice answered. "I was there and I didn't see anything—certainly no aboriginal vengeance-seeker. Just the good, pleasant folk of Clear Creek."

Like Jack Troll. But Troll was the one man who couldn't have done it. He was outisde trying to beat Ruff's brains out when the killing took place.

"What about this?" the colonel asked, and from his top desk drawer he removed an envelope. Inside was the Spanish coin. It lay on the worn wood of the colonel's desk, gleaming dully.

"It's old."

"A motive for murder?"

Ruff shrugged. "I've seen men killed for a nickel. If there happened to be quite a few of those . . ."

"You think there might be? How about this, Ruffin?" the colonel asked, leaning back in his chair and clasping his hands behind his head. "Hickam was digging in what he thought was an Indian burial site and came across a horde of Spanish treasure?"

"You really should consider those dime novels, Colonel."

MacEnroe held up a hand. "I know, I know, but it's possible, isn't it?"

"I've only ever heard of one expedition coming this far north. A priest called Father Aguilar. Looking for converts to the faith. If I recall . . ."

"Yes?" the colonel asked patiently.

"If I recall, there's no record as to what happened to them after leaving Colorado. The assumption was that Indians got them."

"Hickam's Indians?"

Ruff was silent, thinking it over. At last he shrugged. "You've got me. I don't think anyone actually knows if Aguilar got this far north. During the winter? Seems to me someone found some armor and a piece of a wooden cross, and someone back East made that guess."

"It wasn't someone," the colonel said, playing his trump. "It was Hickam."

"Enjoyed that, didn't you, sir?" Justice asked.

The colonel said, "I guess I did. The truth is that Clive Hickam wrote up the theories I was just giving you. He wasn't given a lot of support. It seems he was laughed out of one scientific forum. They said Aguilar couldn't have made it this far north, said anyway that the Sioux hadn't yet drifted into the area, and if there was an aboriginal people along the Heart, no one had found any evidence of it. Hickam meant to."

"I see. So he came west to vindicate his theories."

"So it seems."

"And got himself killed—maybe there's something to your cache-of-gold idea. Maybe someone just didn't care for Doctor Clive Hickam."

"Could be. He seems to have rubbed a lot of people the wrong way in Clear Creek. He was a man who needed to be right about everything."

"Well, I'm sorry the man's dead, but I doubt we'll ever find out what happened."

The colonel smiled again and Justice didn't like it. "I hope we will find out—that's what Regiment wants."

"Regiment?"

"General Studdard. On orders. Technically Hickam was under army protection when he was murdered. The territory itself is under military jurisdiction. General Studdard wants a special investigator put on this."

Justice wasn't answering the colonel's smile now. He liked it better when the colonel was in a foul mood, as he had been when Justice came in. Ruff had thought it was the whiskey that had brightened his outlook. It wasn't.

"Who?" Ruff asked warily.

"Someone who knows the country, knows the people of Clear Creek, knows the Indians, and has some background in the history of the territory—enough to know about Father Aguilar, for instance."

"Damn it all," Justice muttered. "Said too much, didn't I?"

"You were my choice anyway." The colonel decided to have another short drink. "As of now, consider yourself a special investigator. And, Ruff, let me know if you come up with anything I can use in a dime novel."

Justice bit his tongue to keep from answering the

first thing that came to mind. "When do I start? Now?"

"A day or two. We're waiting for a Doctor Clark to arrive from Minneapolis. He'll proceed to the site with you."

"Who's he? Another scientist?"

"Hickam's assistant, apparently."

"Good—I needed a civilian along. Does anyone realize Stone Eyes is still out there?"

"I don't know. Hopefully that won't be true for long. I'm sending Lieutenant Sly out in the morning to reconnoiter and if possible engage the Sioux force. If he reports back that Stone Eyes has drifted out of the area again, the people of Clear Creek will be moving back—to what, I don't know. The town was pretty well destroyed."

"They'll go back," Ruff guessed. "At least some of them. Maybe the man who killed Clive Hickam. The man who thinks there's still more gold out there waiting."

"It's not exactly going to be a cakewalk, is it, Ruff?"

"They seldom are, sir. Is there some reason I always draw these assignments?"

"Sure. I like you, Ruffin." And the colonel, damn him, was smiling again.

Justice retrieved his hat without another word and went out, slamming the door. Fort Abraham Lincoln's first sergeant looked up from his paperwork and asked, "The old man still in a bad mood, is he?"

"No, Mack, he isn't. I only wish to hell he was."

The colonel's laugh rang from inside his office and Justice crossed the orderly room, going out with another bang. Sergeant Mack Pierce stared at the closed door for a long minute, then shrugged massively and got back to work.

Justice crossed to the sutler's store and equipped

himself for a week out on the plains. There might or might not be any town of Clear Creek nearby to resupply him in the next few days. Goods of any kind were sure to be scarce anyway. Stone Eyes had likely taken everything he could and destroyed half of the rest.

Justice spent the rest of that day fishing beneath an agreeable cottonwood tree beside the sunlit Missouri, and most of the next day sleeping. By then Sly's patrol had gone out and had returned: negative contact. The Delaware scout, Ka-lak, had decided that the raiding Sioux were drifting north once more, toward the Canuck border.

That lit a fire under the people of Clear Creek.

"I'm getting back there tomorrow. I'm damned if some squatter is going to move onto my property. I'm protecting whatever I've got left from white raiders now that the red ones are gone," a Clear Creek resident declared.

But Jenny Farnsworth wasn't really concerned. She was only concerned about losing Ruff Justice, and she was working hard to prevent that.

She was smooth and lithe and full-breasted and eager. Justice hovered over her in his hotel room, looking into her eyes, which glowed softly as he lowered his naked body against hers, into hers. She shuddered, made a pleased sound, and clenched his buttocks suddenly, wildly, drawing him in, holding him there.

"There's no one at Clear Creek, no one but Jake Troll," she said, and tears of self-pity welled up in her youthful eyes. She paused to say, "A littler slower. Right there—that's good, very good." Ruff agreed, although there was a little too much chatter to suit him.

"I know my father's going to make me marry Jake.

Oh, Justice!" She lifted herself from the bed, her back arching, her lips finding his mouth, working hungrily against it.

"He's probably got his good points," Ruff said. He didn't want to talk about Jake Troll or Jenny Farnsworth's troubles, however: he wanted to go on doing what he was doing in relative silence—penetrating the active, eager young woman, feeling her cling to him, all legs and arms and willing mouth.

"He drinks," she nearly panted. Her breath wasn't coming regularly now. Her head rolled from side to side as her hips lifted and nudged Ruff's pelvis in a constant, primitive rhythm. "Drinks a lot."

"I know."

"Harder now—God, Justice, again. Push again!" She seemed lost in her sensuality, but Jenny Farnsworth was a woman capable of concentrating on two things at once, it seemed. "You don't drink, do you? Not at all?"

Ruff almost heard her. His body was doing his thinking for him now, answering Jenny's rhythm, adding to it. Tearing at her body, his hands filled with the full firm globes of her breasts as he felt the need in his loins turn into accomplishment and he finished with a rush that caused Jenny Farnsworth to gurgle with pleasure, with a sense of her own accomplishment.

She lay there beneath him, stroking his back, going on about Jake Troll and how he had knocked down the only suitable man in all of Clear Creek, Henry Travis, over her, on the front porch of the schoolhouse, for God's sake, while her best friend Susan Cribbs from the Triple C Ranch down south had to watch it. And Henry Travis ran away with a bloody nose while Troll cussed at him, and when her father walked out of the schoolhouse, where they were having the box lunch social, he didn't so much as lift his voice to Jake, who was dead—that is to say, dead drunk all the time. . . .

The rock crashing through the hotel-room window was almost a relief. Ruff rolled from the bed, motioning to Jenny to remain there. As the girl sat up, wide-eyed and wondering, Justice crossed to where his gun belt hung from the chair, and went back to the window, moving carefully over the broken glass.

"Who is it?" the girl asked in a frightened whisper.

"Can't see." Ruff parted the curtain slightly with his gun barrel and peered out into the dark alley below his window. He saw no one and then he did: Jake Troll, staggering from the alley mouth farther up with a bottle in one hand, a big navy Colt in the other.

The man was going to have to be taught another lesson. One he would remember this time.

3

Ruff Justice was wearing his buckskin pants and no boots when he slipped out of the hotel's side door and into the chilly darkness of the alley behind the hotel. Steam rose from his lips as he edged his way down the alley, one hand on the rough walls of the building there, the other holding his Colt revolver loosely at his side. He had no intention of shooting Troll—who was either stupidly stubborn or drunk or both—but Troll himself was carrying a weapon and you don't have to be smart or sober to pull the trigger of a gun.

Ruff glanced up at his hotel-room window. It was just a dark eye staring back at the night. At least Jenny had had the sense to turn the lamp out.

"Justice!" a slurred voice roared. Ruff's mouth tightened. It was Troll, roaring drunk, angry.

A crash of bottles and tin cans and the muttered curse that followed let Justice know that Troll had just stumbled into a pile of trash. Ruff stopped next to the back door of the stable, arms folded across his bare chest, waiting.

Eventually Troll would find his way down the alley. No sense in the both of them stumbling around out there.

It took another three or four minutes before Troll

came into sight again, staggering so badly that one shoulder caromed off the wall of the feed store beside him. He still had his gun and his bottle with him, but he didn't look as if he knew which was which anymore.

"Justice," Troll yelled again, looking up. "Come to kill you."

It was all drunken bragging—a last-ditch, childish effort on Troll's part to bolster his apparently fragile manhood. There was a little boy locked up in that hulking body, one who was frightened and maybe disturbed. It didn't mean that he couldn't kill.

Ruff waited, moving into deeper shadows where the hayloft dock above cut out the starlight. Once Troll got past him, Justice meant to move in behind him and disarm him or cold-cock him with the Colt.

It didn't happen that way.

Behind Justice the stable door opened a crack, creaking on unoiled iron hinges, and the pistol from inside stabbed flame at the darkness of the alley. Justice wheeled and fired, going to his knee as a second shot spattered him with dirt from the alley floor.

Justice's Colt spoke four times in rapid, deadly succession, sending lead through the planks of the stable door and tearing splinters from the weathered wood, bringing a cry of agony from within.

Troll, turning dumbly at the sounds of gunfire, found himself covered by Ruff's big blue revolver.

"Drop it, Troll, or you're dead," Justice said, his voice raspy, deep.

The bottle went first, smashing against a rock. Then the big fist unclenched and the pistol dropped. Eyeing the stable door, Ruff moved to where Troll waited, and kicked the pistol into the darkness.

"What?" Troll's eyes showed a tangle of emotions, all of them blurred by alcohol.

"Move to the stable. I want to look inside and I want you in front of me," Justice said.

"Me?" Troll stammered. He looked exactly like a little boy now—a huge, red-bearded little boy. "Someone with a gun's in there."

"Someone with a gun is out here. Me. And I won't miss."

"Justice," the voice was pleading now. Ruff wasn't feeling merciful.

"Move it, Troll." The hammer on the big single-action Colt came back with an authoritative and menacing click as it ratcheted home. "Now!" Justice's voice had softened, but the threat in it hadn't. Troll nodded dumbly and started toward the stable door.

When Troll hesitated, Justice nudged him politely with the barrel of the Colt. "Don't you want to see your partner?" Ruff asked.

"I swear to you, Justice, I don't know who's in there." Troll was sobering fast, his fear returning sharply.

"I don't believe you."

"Why would I have someone with me? Why should I?"

"Because you're a little man, Troll, and you haven't got the guts to do it on your own."

"That's a lie! I wouldn't—"

"You wouldn't come looking for me in the middle of a night with a loaded gun, would you?"

"I wouldn't have done it," Troll said, swallowing hard. "I wouldn't have shot you."

"Of course not. Not unless you got the chance. Move it, Troll, damn you, or I'll shoot you where you stand, and I'll get away with it too. You men tried to ambush me."

Troll started to say something but couldn't quite get the protest out. His lips moved mutely, and with his hulking shoulders hunched in surrender, he moved to the stable door.

"Open it," Justice commanded.

"There's a man with a gun in there!"

"I don't think he can use it anymore. Let's find out. Open it, damn you or I'll open you up with a forty-four slug."

That encouraged Troll enough to put his hand on the stable door and swing it open. Inside the door was a shock of long splinters splayed out in all directions from the bullets Ruff had put through it.

There were even a few splinters in the face of the man who lay on the floor in a pool of his own dark blood.

"Jesus," Troll gasped.

"No. It's someone else. What's the matter, Troll? Don't like seeing them dead? That could've been me, you idiot. That makes me mad, Troll, mad enough to whip your fat ass."

"I didn't—"

"Look at him, Troll," Ruff said, jerking the big man around by the shoulder. "That could have been me. I wouldn't like to think of myself going out that way. The head wound—took out his eyes. See that—" Ruff's toe touched some semiliquid substance next to the skull. "All that's left of his brain. I wouldn't like that to be me, Troll. I don't like people who want to do it to me."

Troll didn't answer. He turned away and was sick on the stable floor, making a mess of his clothes. The whiskey and the dead man hadn't gone well together.

Justice glanced at Troll in disgust, crouched down, and started going over the body with one hand, finding little. "Who is he?" Ruff wanted to know.

"No idea . . ." Troll wiped his hand nervously

across his lips. "I swear to you I was alone tonight. I get these ideas sometimes."

"Yeah, I know all about your ideas."

Ruff nearly believed Troll now and in another moment he found that he believed him completely. Something small and round and flat was inside the ambusher's shirt pocket.

"What's that?" Troll asked as Ruff held it up to the starlight.

"A piece of silver," Ruff said, but it wasn't. It was Judas money, all right, but it was pure gold. Spanish and very old.

"Go home," Ruff said to Troll.

"Justice, believe me—"

"Damn you, get out of here. Get out of my sight before I put you down beside this one." Ruff had had enough of Troll, too much of him. The big man didn't waste any time getting out of the stable, and when he was gone, Ruff Justice was left alone with the dead man.

With the dead man who had been carrying Spanish gold, just like Clive Hickam had been doing. . . . Justice didn't like it and he didn't understand it. Too bad the man hadn't lived awhile longer.

Had he come on his own, with Troll, or had he just happened to see Troll—maybe he'd overheard him in some saloon—and realized that he had just the ticket, a decoy to distract Justice while he gunned him down?

Ruff went over the body once more, finding nothing. Then, wiping back his hair, he crossed the quiet stable, smelling the horses, the straw, the manure. He went out the front door carefully, closing it behind him. Then, he circled back toward the hotel on bare feet. It hadn't been a hell of a good night. Maybe Jenny Farnsworth could keep her mouth shut long enough to make it better.

The hotel was dead silent as Ruff climbed the stairs again, opened the door to his room, and went in.

Jenny Farnsworth, dressed now, was standing by the dark window. Ruff dropped his trousers and started toward her.

"Can you stand on your hands by any chance?" Justice asked, and Jenny turned sharply.

But it wasn't Jenny Farnsworth. Ruff had never seen this woman before. She had on a long gray skirt, a gray jacket and hat. Under the hat her hair was bound up severely. She wore spectacles that caught the starlight glare, erasing any expression in them.

Ruff didn't need to see her eyes to guess her expression. Her mouth was tightly pinched, the tendons on her throat standing taut.

"Who," she asked, "in the name of all that's sacred are you?"

"Wrong room?" Justice suggested, retreating a little toward his pants. If the woman was worried about his being naked and ready for Jenny Farnsworth's lovemaking, she didn't show it in any way.

"Not according to what I was told—it's dark in here, turn on the lamp. *After* you've put on your pants, please. Disgusting. I hope, pray you are not who I fear you are." With fading hope she asked, "Ruffin T. Justice?"

"Guilty."

"I imagine so—frequently."

"Whenever possible," Justice cracked, but the lady wasn't about to smile. Ruff had his pants on and had grabbed for his shirt. Before putting it on he struck a match and lit the lamp.

By the light he saw that the woman was young, possibly attractive in a bound, severe, and distinctly unappealing way. Her eyes were actually green—a disapproving green.

"Ruff Justice," she said. It seemed to be a bad-tasting name. "I was afraid so."

"Where's Jenny?"

"If you are referring to a short little girl with massive breasts, she fled when shots were fired in the alley. Was that you? It must have been, I suppose, out killing your hardy enemies. Or just on a toot."

She leaned against the wall, hands clasped in front of her in what might have been an unconscious defensive gesture: two folded, white fists before her virginal crotch.

Ruff pulled on his shirt, ran his fingers through his hair, and sat on the rumpled bed.

"School out?" he asked.

"I beg your pardon?" she said in a metallic voice.

"You must be a schoolmarm."

"A schoolteacher—hardly. I am Doctor Jan Clark, and I was told you were expecting me. I didn't think it was too late for a visit. There seems to be a lot of activity in this town yet, over on the main street—whatever the name of it is. All sorts of drunken cowboys and soldiers screeching, acting like savages—"

"Jan Clark," Ruff repeated, ignoring the brief and irrelevant moral crusade.

"Yes, Doctor Clark."

"From Minneapolis," Justice said unhappily.

"Correct again. You do recall being informed that I was en route to the frontier, then?"

Ruff shook his head and lay back on the bed, one knee propped up, hands behind his head. The lady's mouth tightened still more as she studied him, obviously not liking what she saw.

"Yes, I recall. I was told that a Doctor Clark was arriving, Clive Hickam's assistant, an archaeologist. I just didn't realize—"

"Oh, I understand," she snapped, waving a frustrated hand that hovered overhead for a while like a great white butterfly. "You're one of the ancient type of hunter-man who thinks a woman can work only in a school or perhaps in a bank. You think there's no other place for a female."

"There's a few others," Justice said. He glanced at the bed and the already colorless face of the eastern professor turned chalk-white.

"That's about what I'd expect from you," she said, biting off each word.

Ruff grinned. "Good, then you're not disappointed."

"People like you, Mister Justice, always disappoint me."

Ruff answered, "And people like you disappoint me, Miss Clark—do you know why? You've got nothing to do but go around making hasty moral judgments, quick assessments. You have a point of view and obviously that's the only correct one. Everyone else is obviously wrong. You propagandize yourselves. Fine—do whatever you want, think whatever you want."

"I assure you I intend to."

"But you don't belong here. Not in Dakota," Ruff went on. "This is earth-and-sky country, blood and flesh, and fire."

"Very poetic—"

"And a man has to be different here," Justice interrupted. "So does a woman."

"I didn't come here as a woman; I came as a scientist, hoping to do a decent piece of work."

"That wraps it up," Justice said.

"I don't understand you."

"I go everywhere as a man. A real woman goes everywhere with her womanhood."

"I can't see what possible relevance this has to the reason for my trip to Dakota."

"None, I suppose. I like to shoot my mouth off now and then," Justice said. "Just like most other people." The look he gave her was steady and searching. She didn't like it, didn't like those blue eyes or the lean body of this man.

"I am expected to travel on the prairie with you?"

"You were. Talk to the colonel. Maybe he can find you a human being to go with."

"That," Dr. Jan Clark said, rising to her full height of five-foot-one, "is exactly what I intend to do. I hope—I hope the colonel chastises you!"

She went out then, her long gray skirt swishing around her ankles, and slammed the door. Ruff Justice lay grinning on the bed. Then after a while a yawn conquered that expression and he just lay there wondering where Jenny Farnsworth had run off to.

He wondered about the killer with the Spanish doubloon in his pocket.

He spent more time wondering about Jenny Farnsworth. Maybe she talked too much, but her conversation was a hell of a lot more pleasant than that of the scientist lady. Ruff put her out of his mind completely.

The lady seemed to have a lot of pull and she would use it now. Go to MacEnroe and tell him what a savage Justice was. It suited Ruff Justice fine.

Although he wondered—wondered just what was going on down at the ancient burial site, if that was what it was. Wondered what *had* gone on there, hundreds of years ago when Father Aguilar had trekked north across the breadth of the continent seeking converts—and carrying Spanish gold.

4

The colonel wasn't going to be reasonable. His sense of humor, displayed on Justice's last visit, was completely gone. The whiskey bottle was gone.

The scientist, in buckskin skirt and pale-green cotton blouse was there, sitting in the corner, her mouth clamped shut, her green eyes sparking behind her bifocals.

"We can't discuss this," the colonel said firmly. "It's Ruff Justice or no one."

"Sir—" Ruff began in protest.

"Shut up, Ruffin," MacEnroe said in a tone completely unlike his usual voice.

"Colonel," the woman pleaded, leaning forward, hands clasped on her lap, neck straining toward the commanding officer of Fort Lincoln, "I cannot go out on the plains with this—man. No decent woman could."

"Then stay here," MacEnroe said.

"In case you have forgotten, Colonel," the woman said, huffing up, "General Studdard himself wrote the letter on your desk, the letter that requests that you provide protection and assistance to me."

"I assure you I haven't forgotten anything," MacEnroe said stiffly. "Nor would General Studdard allow me to. You fail to appreciate the situation here, however."

"Do I?" She glanced at Justice, who smiled, and the woman's head turned away angrily.

MacEnroe was looking at them as if they were two spoiled children. He took a slow breath between his teeth and went on.

"I cannot send an army patrol with you, Doctor Clark. For one thing, we have had a series of renegade incidents at the Pine Ridge Reservation. I'm sending a company of soldiers up there to reenforce reservation Indian police. Second, we have Stone Eyes somewhere north of us, perhaps as far as the Canadian border, but still within my area of responsibility. There's no one we want right now more than Stone Eyes. Red Cloud, Sitting Bull, Crazy Horse—all the great chiefs are far less dangerous."

"Aren't those men the war leaders of the savages?" Jan Clark asked.

"They are, were, but they've taken refuge in Canada and apparently mean to stay there. Also those men are intelligent men, and I think basically good men. Men on the other side of our war, but men who care for their people, for saving lives.

"Stone Eyes wants to take lives," the colonel concluded.

"General Studdard—"

"General Studdard understands priorities, Doctor. I'm sure he offered you all possible assistance, as I mean to, but when it comes to the security of the people on the prairie and escorting one person on a scientific expedition, the general knows which choice I need to make. My forces are thin, and so far as we know, Clear Creek is a trouble-free area at the moment—the citizens of that community are on their way back home."

"Still," the doctor said, "there must be someone besides *this* man."

"I have an Indian scout named Ta-show. He doesn't speak except in sign language, however."

"An officer—" the woman began.

"All of my officers—and I'm short two junior officers just now—are needed in other areas. I could send you with an enlisted man, not a top sergeant, but I don't think you would find them much more satisfactory."

"Anyone would be," she said tightly.

"None of them knows the land like Justice does. From here to Clear Creek all you have to do is follow wagon ruts. From there on it's a different story. Justice knows where the burial site is. Besides," the colonel said with a sigh—the officer didn't like to have to do so much explaining; he generally gave orders and his orders were carried out—"I have already appointed Justice investigator into the murder of Clive Hickam. He will go to Clear Creek; he will find out what, if anything, is going on at the burial site—if that really does exist. He will find the murderer of your colleague. And, if it's necessary, Justice is capable of taking care of a murderer."

"Or a drunk in an alley," the professor said in a self-satisfied way.

Justice ignored that remark. The colonel ignored it. MacEnroe informed her, "That's the way it has to be. Otherwise, you may just as well go back and lodge a complaint with General Studdard."

"Looks like we're stuck with each other," Justice said, examining the fingernails of his right hand.

"So it appears," she answered in the coldest voice Justice had heard for a long while. "Tell me, Colonel"—she glanced at Justice once—"where can a woman buy a pistol and find someone to show her how to use it?"

She did it, too. The next time Ruff saw Jan Clark she was wearing a little pearl-handled chrome-plated Remington .32 pistol. Whether she'd gotten anyone to show her how to fire the little double-action pistol was something Ruff figured he could do without knowing.

The lady had hired or purchased a buckboard, and the back of it was filled with bedrolls, tinned goods, picks, shovels, a surveyor's transit, rope, and a variety of unnamed, apparently useless implements. She also had a load of seasoned firewood. Justice looked it over dubiously.

"Well? Did I do something to dissatisfy the great plainsman and womanizer?"

Ruff hesitated a minute to let her know he appreciated sarcasm when he heard it. "The firewood," he responded eventually. "Dump it."

"We'll need it."

"No."

"I've inquired, Mister Justice, and I know there aren't a hundred living trees between here and Clear Creek. Let alone deadwood."

"We use buffalo chips in this part of the country, Miss Clark."

"*Doctor* Clark . . ." She blinked after her automatic correction and asked, "We use what?"

"Buffalo chips."

"And what, pray tell, are those?"

"We got 'em scattered across the plains. Hundreds of years of 'em."

"But what are they?"

"Can you imagine a buffalo's tail, *Miss* Clark?" Justice asked.

"Why, yes, but . . . Oh."

"Yes. Just lower your thoughts a tad."

"That's disgusting, revolting," the woman said.

"It beats the hell out of trying to carry a couple of

cords of wood around, seeing if you can't break down your team or an axle. As a matter of fact, you made a second mistake in buying this light buckboard. An ox cart would have suited better, considering the load you seem to be carrying. What is all of that gear anyway?"

"I'm sure," she sniffed, "you wouldn't understand a scientist's equipment."

"No. I'm just a buffalo-chip-burning country boy," Justice said. "And a womanizer."

It might have been his imagination, but it seemed that Jan Clark's hand dropped toward her new security talisman, the pearl-handled .32 that rode on the holster turned slightly toward the front of her skirt.

"Scare you?" he asked with a smile.

"You couldn't do a blessed thing to scare me, Mister Justice."

He answered soberly, "I won't. I promise you that. Even a womanizer has his limits."

She declined to respond to that remark—a remark Justice wasn't particularly proud of. One thing you don't do in this world is attack a man's pride. Or a woman's. It's something they don't forgive easily, and Justice had done it twice in two days. To Troll and to the lady scientist. Neither was likely to forget soon.

They rolled out of Fort Lincoln just before noon. Justice let the lady drive her own rig, which she was almost competent at, while he straddled his little dun pony, the one with a single blue eye. No bigger than an Indian pony, the horse was named Scalawag, and was tough as a mountain cat and damned near as mean. It could run all day, eat all night, thank you for a rubdown and a scoop of oats by taking a chunk out of your leg or biting off your ear. Justice had favored big horses for a long while, ever since he had taken that great Appaloosa from the Nez Percé when the Crow and their enemies had fought the bitter struggle.

The bigger the horse, the better on the plains. The Indians' runty ponies couldn't match a well-grained, strapping army-regulation bay for endurance or speed. It was an unrecognized, very crucial factor in the plains wars. Justice had always ridden the big animals.

But this damned dun with its threatening blue eye and its nasty temper could run with the best of them, and more. It seemed to have no bottom at all. Justice had spent eighteen hours in the saddle during a very close race with death, and Scalawag hadn't stumbled, faltered, or even lathered.

He didn't like the horse, but damn all, he respected it.

His feelings about the woman who rode behind him in the spring buckboard were slightly different. But he supposed you couldn't expect much from a woman who had gone to an eastern college.

The day passed lazily. Yellow sun in a deep-blue sky, scattered puffball clouds, the long grass shifting in the wind. They spotted pronghorn leaping away in the distance, jackrabbits, and once a small—almost pitifully small—herd of buffalo. There was nothing unique about the day. Ruff Justice watched the horizon as he always had, looking for the unexpected Sioux or renegade Cheyenne; he watched for game, spotted his landmarks. Beneath Scalawag's hooves the grass bent and showed silver in the sun. The buckboard followed the ruts carved into the prairie's face by the many wagons that had rolled west and were even now rolling back to Clear Creek.

There was nothing unique about it. Nothing spectacular in the rising of meadowlarks from the long grass, in the sweeping flow of the wind, in the distant sailing crows or the sudden flash of a cottontail.

Nothing at all unique—it was simply exquisite, free, empty, and beautiful, broadening the life and mind of a man just to look upon it.

Justice couldn't get enough of it, of freedom and enormity, any more than he could grow tired of desert and purple mountains, a thousand square miles of snow forest.

Dr. Jan Clark had had enough of the prairie in fifty miles. Her bottom was sore, her hands were growing blistered from the reins, her eyes were red and raw from squinting into the sun.

"When are we going to stop, for mercy's sake?" she shouted to Justice, who was riding ahead and fifty feet to the north. He half-turned, resting a hand on the cantle of his saddle.

"Whenever you want, lady. It's your schedule."

"When *do* you eat out here?" she demanded sharply. The heat and the traveling weren't doing wonders for her already acid temperament.

"Usually," Ruff Justice drawled, "when we get hungry."

The lady smothered a reply. She saw something ahead that interested her and she pointed almost eagerly. "On that knoll. There's a tree there. Shade," she said as if nothing could be more desirable. It wasn't much wonder. She wore a narrow-brimmed hat, and the buckboard had no canvas top. The lady scientist had yet to learn there were reasons for things being done in a certain way.

Ruff grunted something and turned the dun toward the hillock. The old oak there was twisted, stolid, and gray. Justice reached the spot half a mile ahead of the lady and he swung down to stare southward and westward, holding the reins to the dun, which had found a patch of dry grama grass to graze on.

He could see the Heart River, silver and narrow, the folded hill hiding Clear Creek, and the distant, hazy mountains. There was nothing else. No smoke, no Indian sign at all, and that pleased Justice greatly. He had tangled with Stone Eyes before and had no wish to do it again.

He turned at the sound of the approaching buckboard. The axles were whining and Justice wondered if the lady had bothered to have the wheels greased. He guessed the answer would be no—he also decided not to ask her if she had a bucket of grease. She took each question as if it were a challenge.

Ruff broke out his lunch gear: a tin of apricots, jerky, coffee. He started a small fire and sat close to it, putting his coffeepot on to boil.

The lady stepped down gingerly, rubbing her flank when she thought Justice wasn't looking. Walking to the fire, she stood looking down at him.

"That's not much of a meal."

"It'll keep me until suppertime," Justice said.

"Will we make Clear Creek by nightfall?"

"No," the scout told her. "In the morning."

"I see." She didn't like it, but she couldn't change time or geography. Slowly Jan Clark returned to her wagon, climbed up awkwardly, her boot slipping, and started digging through her too methodically packed goods for something to eat. By the time she had come back, Ruff had had the single cup of coffee he wanted.

"Now I . . ." the scientist began. Her eyes widened behind her spectacles as Ruff poured the dregs of his coffee onto his fire, putting it out.

"Why did you do that?"

"Were you going to cook?"

"You know I was," Jan Clark insisted.

"No," Ruff said dryly. "I didn't. I just didn't want my fire to spread. Fire on the prairie is a terrible thing. You were gone so long I thought you'd plain decided not to eat."

"And now what am I supposed to do?"

"Got a match?" Justice asked.

"Somewhere . . ." Justice handed her one from his waterproof tin.

"You're welcome," the tall man said. The lady was furious, but trying to hold it in.

"This is not what I would expect from the man who is supposed to be my trail guide. However, I suppose I can start my own fire."

"I suppose so. Just collect a little fuel," Justice told her.

The lady, suddenly horrified, looked around. "Oh, collect those—things."

"If you want a fire."

"I suppose you think this is all very funny, Justice. But I've never found it amusing for a person to be simply obnoxious. And if you think I won't collect some of those buffalo things, you're wrong."

Her voice had begun to rise sharply. Justice, suddenly bored, looked off into the distances. Only out of the corner of his eye did he see the lady gingerly kicking at and then reluctantly gathering dry buffalo chips for her fire.

It took her most of an hour to get enough fire to cook over, still more time to scrounge up an iron skillet, dump her tinned beef into it, and brew herself some tea. But if she would rather prove a point than hurry on to Clear Creek, it was fine with Justice. He didn't care for the woman or the assignment.

The afternoon was short. Ruff held up at a creek crossing and waited for the buckboard to arrive.

"What now?" the lady asked, peevishly.

"We'd do best to hold up here where we've got water and grass for the horses."

"There's an hour of daylight left."

"Very true. We don't know for sure if there's water an hour on," Justice explained patiently.

"Well, all right." She seemed to be agreeing just because her butt was sore from being slapped by that wagon seat all day as the buckboard bounced over the plains.

When she climbed down and stood looking at the horses, it was obvious she didn't know what to do about unhitching them. Ruff unsaddled Scalawag first, rubbed him down a little, and left him to drink before he sauntered back to unharness the team in front of the lady's belligerent gaze.

"You're very helpful," she said haughtily. She stood with hands on hips, the sundown light glinting on her spectacles, the wind shifting the long skirt she wore.

"So are you," Justice said without stopping his work.

"What does that mean?"

"Nothing at all. Just a fact. You'd be surprised how much help a good woman can be to a man out here. One that can take care of horses, start a fire, and cook."

"You ought to take yourself a squaw," the doctor said.

Ruff just half-turned and lowered his eyelids a little. There was something in his expression Jan Clark didn't understand. Ruff Justice didn't tell her. He didn't tell her that he had taken a squaw once, a Crow woman who was a joy to be with, who laughed and worked and collected firewood and trapped and warmed his bed at night. A woman who was a woman and not some sort of icon with a petrified womb willing to sit back and make judgments on life and men without ever knowing what either was about.

"I'll water your team. If you want a campfire, either start one or wait till I get back."

"You'll let me share your fire tonight?" the scientist asked with mock surprise and pleasure. "How kind of you, Mister Justice." She touched her breast and tilted toward him slightly. "How very kind of you to do your job."

Ruff didn't answer. He didn't think it was amusing for a person to be simply obnoxious either. Maybe that was a point in common.

Sunset turned the little stream gold and orange. The horses drank and occasionally lifted their muzzles. Beads of sundown-jeweled water trickled from them.

Ruff thought he was imagining it at first, but when he turned his head, there was a curl of smoke rising from a pile of buffalo chips the lady had built. He could see her glaring at him from behind the veil of smoke, and he turned away before she saw the thin smile developing.

Walking the horses back, he picketed them on the grass and went to the fire. The lady was crouched down, holding a cup of coffee balanced on one knee.

"Proud of me?" she asked, nodding at the fire.

"Sharing that coffee?" Ruff asked without answering.

She hesitated, seemed to soften a little, and nodded.

Ruff poured a cup and squatted opposite her, sipping at it.

"I suppose you're feeling smug," Jan Clark said. "Having taught the eastern lady a lesson, showing her how to get her hands dirty."

"Smug? Over teaching somebody how to survive, or

trying to? No. Let me explain something, lady, you're going to a wilderness area alone. You plan on staying down at that so-called burial site with no one around for a hundred miles. You didn't know how to start a damned campfire. There's so much else you don't know that I don't have the time to begin to teach you.

"You're going to be isolated and cold and scared and lonely. If a snake bites you, you're going to have to tend to it yourself. If you come across a prowling cougar, you're going to have to handle it. I won't be there. I hope to hell someone showed you how to shoot that little peashooter of a pistol you're carrying, though I don't know what good it's going to do you against a bear or a wandering renegade Indian, or against the people—and there seem to be some—who want to look that site over carefully for gold."

"Gold." That was the only part that got through and the lady's face seemed to pale a little. It was now dusk, and the sky was deep purple, the firelight dancing and weaving in the breeze. "How did you know about that?"

"A Spanish coin was found next to Clive Hickam's body. How could it be much of a secret?"

"No one was supposed to know. Even in the paper Doctor Hickam was preparing he didn't mention the gold by name. He simply said he had found incontrovertible evidence that Father Aguilar had made it this far north." Her voice had grown weaker and she was just a little unnerved.

"It's no secret about the gold. I know. The colonel knows. Every man and woman in Clear Creek knows. What's the matter, did you think you were the only one who knew? Is that why you came out alone to Dakota?"

She didn't answer or look at him, and Ruff Justice, silently sipping his coffee, began to wonder. Had she come for the sake of science or was it the lure of gold? There was something working in the back of the lady's mind, something that seemed to pass behind her eyes and cloud them. It was disappointment and perhaps a touch of fear.

Maybe she was thinking about gold or maybe she had just remembered something else. Hickam had been murdered. It was just possible that she was walking into a situation where the same thing could happen to her, college degree or no.

There was still someone out there who had taken a twisted arrow and driven it into Clive Hickam's body.

Someone who killed.

When they rolled up in their blankets well apart, the fire burning low and then sputtering out, Justice lay awake for a long while watching the stars. Somewhere a long way off, a prairie wolf set up a deep howl that echoed across the plains. Ruff glanced at the sleeping scientist. Her body gave a little shudder and Justice thought she was awake, that the sound of the wolf had frightened her.

Neither assumption was correct. He rose and walked silently to her, discovering that she was asleep. Her body twitched again, and crouching down, Justice saw that she was crying—crying in her sleep, tears running from her eyes. Without the spectacles her face was attractive, very young and vulnerable.

Ruff grumbled and strode away, angry with himself. He almost liked her better as an obnoxious invulnerable icon of a woman. She didn't have to show herself in her sleep—it just made things more difficult. More difficult to simply dump her down on the Heart and let her figure out for herself what sort of situation she was getting into.

"Damn you, woman," Ruff said softly. "You make me feel like a real bastard."

He lay down again, blanket tugged up to his chin, watching the stars for a little while longer, listening to the wolf and the muted sobbing of the sleeping woman.

Tangled thoughts kept Justice awake until long past midnight—past midnight, when the silently moving shadow of an intruder came between Ruff and the sleeping woman.

5

Ruff Justice held himself still. His hand slowly stretched out and slipped his Colt from its oiled holster, but otherwise he didn't move. He watched and waited.

The intruder who had been only a shadow now took on the blurred outlines of a man, a narrow, slightly hunched man.

He moved away from Justice and hovered for a moment over the sleeping form of the woman. Justice's thumb tightened over the hammer of his Colt. He had started to raise the barrel of the Colt when the stranger, shaking his head, moved away from the woman.

He glanced at Ruff, seemed unconcerned about him and moved on to the buckboard, which stood fifty feet away, star-shadowed and bleak.

Justice only watched. The man hadn't come to kill apparently. What *did* he want?

Ruff never found out. The woman sleeping across from him stirred, rolled over, and then sat up suddenly, her eyes going wide. She reached for and found her pearl-handled pistol.

"Don't!" Justice called, but his voice was drowned out by the report of the gun. Six times the woman pulled the trigger of the little .32, scattering lead all over the landscape as she tried to gun down the intruder, who took to his heels.

One bullet struck an iron strap on the wagon; the others seemed to miss everything in God's creation. Justice was on his feet now, racing after the camp robber.

Jan Clark was on her knees, her hair loose around her shoulders, the empty pistol in her hand, screaming something Justice didn't get.

Justice ran on, his bare feet seeming to find each rock and sticker. He had his Colt in his hand but never got the opportunity to use it.

The intruder simply vanished. He was gone, leaving no sign that Ruff Justice could find in the night. For a long while he stood in the silent darkness, listening. He heard nothing, not the sound of an escaping horse or the fleeing feet of a man. He saw nothing. The night had come and devoured the raider.

Justice started back toward the camp and was confronted by an accusing Jan Clark.

"You let him get away. A killer," she shrieked. Her nerves were shot. The night had whisked away most of her confidence. The night and the empty plains.

"I don't know what he was. He wasn't a killer. He had his chances and didn't take them."

"He was in our camp."

"Yes." Justice studied the woman. By starlight she seemed smaller; without her spectacles she was more of a woman. She wore a nightdress over a skirt, but there was nothing at all under the nightdress where it molded itself to her heaving breasts. The nipples stood taut and interesting, and Justice let his gaze run over her body before the woman turned away in an incensed growl.

"Sorry. It's nature, you know."

47

"In the middle of this . . ." She sputtered something that made no sense at all. Turning, she regained her composure, but she folded her arms over her breasts and kept them there. "Who was it? What did he want?"

"I have no idea," Justice said. "Whoever taught you how to shoot that fancy pistol of yours didn't do a very good job, by the way. It's a wonder you didn't shoot me or a horse, or yourself."

"You never even fired your pistol."

"No, I didn't," Justice admitted. "I've seen too many mistakes made. When I shoot, I want to know who, what my target is."

"Maybe you were in on it with him," the lady scientist said accusingly and quite illogically.

"Sure. We wanted to raid your tinned goods and then use your body. It's all I've had in mind since you seduced me with your gentle femininity."

"Funny. You're oh so funny all the time . . ."

Then the lady just sagged. Her knees went rubbery as the fear and anger drained out of her and she became a small lonely human being walking the earth, afraid of life and of death.

Justice caught her before she collapsed. She clung to him, her fingers kneading his shoulders, a small, terrible moan escaping her lips as the tears broke free of her green eyes.

That lasted all of five seconds. Then, angry with herself, disgusted with Justice, Jan Clark pushed away and walked slowly back to her bed.

By the morning light Justice couldn't find out much more about the interloper of the previous night. Nothing had been disturbed in the wagon—he hadn't had the time. His tracks were soft, indistinct, as if he had had little weight, but Justice thought the prints he had left were made by moccasins.

Jan Clark, looking slightly less stiff and truculent, found Justice crouched over one such footprint.

"Can you tell anything?" she asked hopefully.

"Not from this." Ruff stood and straightened. "Except that he's good, very good. He moves silently and swiftly."

"Perhaps it was an Indian, a wandering Sioux. One of this Stone Eyes' people."

"Maybe. Maybe a hungry wanderer. But he was no killer," Justice said.

"I guess we'll never know," Jan Clark said. She was becoming more of the lady scientist, less of a woman, as the sun rose higher. Her voice was a little brittle when she asked, "Will you hitch my team for me or do I have to figure it out for myself?"

Ruff told her, "We haven't got the time for you to figure it out. There wouldn't be anything left of the horses but skin and bones. I'll give you the same advice I gave you before, though. You'd better learn how to do things. There won't be much help for you down at Twin Buttes."

"I'm sure I can hire someone at Clear Creek," the lady answered.

"Maybe so. Do you really want a man around while you're investigating the burial site?" Ruff paused. "Looking for that gold."

"I am not looking for gold," the lady said, taking on a color that didn't come from the flush of the rising sun against the sky. "I am here to continue Clive Hickam's work. That theory, proven or disproven, will either prop up his reputation or make a darn fool out of him. He was my mentor, my friend, my teacher—I won't let the scientific community laugh at him."

She said it with such fervor that Justice very nearly believed her. Nearly.

"Come on, watch me hitch up," he said. "Tell me, they pay you well, those people at the university?"

"I was on Doctor Hickam's staff. With him gone I really don't have a source of income. The last of what savings I did have I spent on the equipment in this wagon and on transportation west."

"I see," Justice said.

"You don't see." The lady grabbed his arm. "You still think I'm looking for gold. All right, I'll tell you what I never wanted to tell anyone: Doctor Hickam . . . was my father."

"You use a different name."

"I had no choice," Jan Clark said. "I was illegitimate. I only found out when I was almost finished with school. I wanted to know my father, so I attended his lectures. I was the only woman there, of course, and perhaps because of that, he took me under his wing. Eventually the truth came out. He was a good man, a decent man."

"I hear he could be a little snappish."

"Who says that?" Jan demanded.

"The people of Clear Creek."

She touched her hair nervously. "You have to understand. Father was impatient with ignorance. He was a college professor, distracted by his own thoughts. At times he could be a little irascible."

"That's what I just said, isn't it?"

"What difference does it make now?" she asked hotly.

"Maybe none, maybe plenty. You haven't forgotten Clive Hickam was murdered, have you? He might just have made himself an enemy."

"I see," she said, slightly mollified.

"And it's still my duty to find out what exactly did happen. I'd rather think that it was a personal matter than that some Indian tracked him down or some

Spanish ghost. I can deal with an angry citizen of Clear Creek a little better."

"Like this Jake Troll," she suggested.

"Got his name somewhere, did you?"

"I looked into the situation, yes. I wanted to know who I was traveling with, what sort of man you were."

"And?" Ruff prompted.

"And I didn't like what I discovered very much."

"No," Justice said, "I guess you wouldn't."

They hitched up in silence and Ruff, saddling the dun, led them out across the stream toward Clear Creek, marked by faintly seen rising smoke behind the low blue hills.

At noon they arrived at the small settlement. It wasn't much to see just now. There had been a row of four white clapboard houses as you entered the town from the east out of the low oak-studded hills. Now two of them were burned to the ground, another half-burned, the other smudged black, windowless.

Along the main street wagons stood between the rows of burned and battered buildings. The streets were filled with litter left from Stone Eyes' rampage. Women's clothing, cans of lard, broken sacks of flour, nails, shingles, and lumber. Among the debris people searched hopefully as Ruff Justice rode Scalawag up the street, leading the way for the lady in the buckboard.

A few people recognized Justice, one or two raised hands, but for the most part they were preoccupied with their own troubles, as they tried to put their lives back together.

Gil Thomas, who owned the dry-goods store, was already at work painting his building. Dan Woods, the hotel keeper, just stood before his fire-damaged building, staring at the window glass scattered on the boardwalk as if he were incapable of movement.

"Can we eat somewhere?" Jan Clark called to Justice.

"I don't know. Let's have a look. A block down."

Surprisingly, the restaurant was nearly untouched, although the waitress said that the Indian raiders had had tremendous appetites or had carried off a hell of a lot.

"There's not much here, but what we got we'll serve," the woman said. She was short, blond, weary. She scribbled down their order, brought coffee, and wandered off again.

"Now, what?" Jan Clark asked.

"Now we go on through to the Heart. Sleep in town tonight, if you want, and leave in the morning."

Jan hesitated. "I don't want to wait around here."

"That's all right too. I just thought maybe we could rest the horses, see that they had some grain if there's any to be had."

"Justice," the woman paused, looking at her coffee, "they know. The people of this town know about the gold."

"I told you they did. At least about the one coin."

She might not have heard him. "The way they looked at us as we came in—do they know about me?"

"Probably. Word gets around pretty fast."

"I don't like it. I won't have it," she amended. "Am I to expect treasure-hunters down at the Indian site, tramping all around?"

"There'll be some. If there's gold or the promise of it, someone will be looking. You can bet on that."

"I won't have it. The Alpha Cave Civilization site is more important than a handful of gold, assuming there even is any more."

"To you, yes," Ruff agreed, moving his elbows as the waitress returned to serve them a make-do meal of

52

tinned tomatoes, bacon, and bread. Jan Clark watched the waitress as if she were an adversary.

When the blonde had gone, she said, "To *me* it is much more important. To science, to the world of knowledge. It's a missing bit of history, Justice. It has to be protected. Protected from a pack of scavenging gold-hunters."

"I don't see how you're going to do that."

"Won't you do it?" she asked. She removed her spectacles, rubbed the bridge of her nose, and peered at Justice with those slightly myopic green eyes.

Justice shook his head. "No, I won't do it. What could I do? Stand watch with a scattergun while you puttered around digging for artifacts?"

"Very well," she said tightly.

"Very well?"

"Very well. I'll do what needs to be done. I've changed my mind, Justice. I want to spend the night here," Jan Clark announced.

Ruff shrugged. Whatever the lady wanted. He began to eat with some relish, watching those green eyes as he did so, trying to figure out what was going on inside the head of the pretty, sterile lady scientist.

After eating Ruff dropped a dollar on the table and went out to see to the horses. The stable was operating after a fashion.

"All my stock was run off, of course," the hostler, a wiry man with no front teeth, told Justice, "but the building's mostly intact and I got oats. Scorched oats," he added dryly.

"It'll do. Watch the dun, he bites."

"I'll bet he does; he's got that gleam in his eye."

Ruff and the stableman both turned at the sound of approaching horses. Three men—one of them wearing a black rain slicker, though the day was clear and bright—rode into the stable and sat their horses, glowering.

Two of the men had blond mustaches waxed to points and unexpected black eyes. The other had no mustache but had the same lean contours to his face.

The oldest of them swung down and said, "Do the horses. We'll be back."

"It's customary to pay in advance," the hostler said. He smiled but the big man in the rain slicker didn't smile back.

"Do it," was all he said. Then he gave Justice a searching look, turned on his heel, and walked away, the other two men swinging down to join him.

"Friendly, aren't they?" Justice said.

"I heard they get a lot less friendly than that," the stableman said. He seemed to have lost a little color.

"You know them?"

"Heard of them. Just realized who they had to be. That's the MacDonalds. Charlie's the oldest one. His brother's name is Kent. Other one's a cousin of some sort, name of Cannfield."

"Outlaws?"

"If you were from down south a way, you'd know," the hostler said. "I didn't know they were in Dakota, but they've done some work in Colorado and Kansas. I imagine the law's looking for them, but probably not too hard. They just might find them. I'd stay clear of them, friend."

"I will," Ruff said. "I've got enough troubles of my own."

"You and me both. Don't worry about the dun or the team, I'll get right to them."

But Justice noticed he took the outlaws' horses first. Carrying his .56 Spencer repeater in its buckskin sheath, Justice started back up town, past the hammering, sawing, painting, happy, dazed citizens of

Clear Creek. He heard one woman say, "What's the use in it, Harry, they'll be back anyway? Stone Eyes will be back. We should have . . ."

Should have what? Ruff wondered. Stayed east, hired out, moved to California, given up and died? You don't do things that way. You try, and if they knock you down, you just try again.

He checked into the hotel, was given a freshly cleaned room, and lay back on the bed for a time, thinking about his lady scientist, the gold, and the twisted arrow.

Finally, when sunset was already beginning to make itself known as an orange-red glint in his window, Ruff Justice rose with a yawn and went out to do what he had been sent to do.

Find out who had killed Clive Hickam and why.

6

On the way out Ruff stopped by the desk where the sleepy red-eyed man lounged in a leather-covered chair, reading an ancient *Police Gazette*.

"Yes, Mister Justice?"

"Did you give Miss Clark a room this evening?"

"Miss . . . oh, the one signs herself Doctor Clark."

"That's the one," Ruff admitted.

The clerk scratched his head. "I couldn't figure that out. I asked her was she signing in for a doctor. Looked around. Hell, we haven't had a doctor in Clear Creek since Doc Pryor cut his own wrists. Drunk, he was."

Ruff let the man go on, unburdening himself of a load of pent-up gossip. Eventually he turned him back to the subject of Jan Clark.

"Then she says she was the doctor herself. *Female* doctor? Well, hell, a doctor's a doctor, so I welcomed her. Showed her this boil on my back." Ruff got a look at the same boil. "The lady," the clerk said a little sadly, "went off in a huff."

"But she took a room here?"

"Took it and went out again," the clerk affirmed.

"Say where she was going?" Justice asked.

"No, didn't seem to wish to talk to me, Justice. Funny sort of woman, ain't she?"

"Yes, she is." Ruff asked, "Did you know Clive Hickam?"

"Hickam—'nother funny bird. Most uppity, onery man I think I've ever crossed trails with. Well, you know, he was educated, from the East and all. I understand if he don't want to come have Sunday supper with me, but you'd of thought he could spare a little hello. Or don't folks back East these days say hello to each other."

"I wouldn't know. Did he have any particular enemies?" Justice asked.

"Hickam? Don't think anyone knew him well enough to hate him exactly, no more'n anyone knew him well enough to like him, assuming there was anything there to like." The clerk's red eyes altered their expression. "Except maybe May Stansford."

"And who's that?"

"Town conscience, social thinker, started a free library that doesn't get much use—in her own house. That's the clapboard still standing." The man nodded vaguely east. "Used to have temperance meetings and such, poetry readings . . . Say, don't you do that sort of thing? Write poetry, that is?"

"Sometimes," Justice said. "May Stansford knew Hickam, did she?"

"Yeah, she knew him as well as anyone. Heard they used to have tea together or something." The clerk waved a hand in a bemused gesture. "Don't see what people get out of that. Tea on her veranda, they say, and I think they both had some interest in the history of the area."

"Did they now?" Ruff said, his eyebrows raising a little.

"Some theory about the Indians—hell, Justice, I

don't know. They never invited me to none of their pink tea parties." The clerk gave Ruff a man-to-man wink and Ruff smiled. They talked a while longer, but there wasn't much more the man could tell Justice.

By the time Ruff Justice left the hotel it was dusk, deep purple, warm, the air dusty from the day's activities. Uptown there was a lot of noise from the first business to reopen in Clear Creek: the Notorious Saloon.

There were a couple of men hanging around on the saloon's plankwalk; they watched Justice darkly from the shadows of their hat brims. One of them was Charlie MacDonald, still inexplicably wearing his rain slicker. Maybe he was a weather prophet, confidently expecting a storm overnight. Maybe he had a shabby suit on underneath—or nothing at all.

Maybe he had something hidden under that slicker. Like a scattergun. Ruff was inclined toward that bet. MacDonald bulged suspiciously in odd places.

Justice paid no apparent attention to the men. He didn't need any trouble with hard-drinking outlaws. Stepping onto the plankwalk himself a little farther on, he made his way toward May Stansford's house. A light seemed to be burning in a downstairs window. Above the house a massive oak stood sentinel like a protective giant. Stars picked out figures against the night sky. A wind drifting off the low hills worked its way through the streets of Clear Creek, drifting paper and litter before it.

The man in the alley had an ax handle in his hand and he hammered down at Justice's head as the scout passed. Ruff turned and tried ducking away, his arm going up defensively. The ax handle slammed into his shoulder, numbing it and filling Justice's body with fiery pain.

Ruff went down on his back, his arm twitching uselessly as he tried to draw his holstered Colt. Lights flashed behind his eyes and his body arched with pain.

The man with the ax handle stood over Justice, primitive, savage, huge. Ruff had a blurred vision of a broad-shouldered, square-faced man. The ax handle fell again and Justice just managed to roll to one side. The hickory club whipped past his head, thudding against the dust of the street.

Justice kicked out with his boot, heard an *oof* as boot leather sank into a soft belly, and watched the attacker stagger backward.

With his left hand Ruff grabbed for his pistol, the cross-draw bringing up the six-chambered Colt. The gun thundered in his hand, spitting flame and lead at the big man. He must have taken a hit, but maybe not with the left hand doing the shooting. At that range Justice found it hard to believe he had missed, but the hulking attacker gave no sign of it. He simply fled, his heavy feet thumping against the alley as he made his escape, leaving Justice groggy and hurting to lie there a minute longer, trying to clear his head.

Clear Creek wasn't particularly concerned about the shot, which was surprising, considering their recent troubles. A lamp went on in one window and across the street a man stepped out in his nightshirt, looking up and down the street. Aside from that, there was no response at all.

It suited Justice. He lay flat on his back, knees drawn up, shoulder aching, arm still partially paralyzed. He was waiting for the pain, the lights in his head, the nausea, to subside.

Troll. That was Justice's first conclusion. It had to have been Jake Troll, his vendetta uncooled by time and Ruff's warnings.

"Maybe," Justice groaned. He had his Colt across his belly, his head still against the dry earth. Now with a moan and a small grunt of effort he sat up, stared bleakly down at the alley, and after a minute got to his feet to stand woozily, one hand against the wall of the burned-out building next to him.

Did Troll have that kind of nerve? Was he that damned obstinate and stupid?

"Maybe," Justice repeated to himself. Without holstering his gun, he walked a way up the alley, looking for blood and finding none, which astonished him. "Couldn't have missed," he told himself. But then he hadn't been real sharp at that moment. Maybe he had completely missed the big man.

Searching slowly by the dim light of the stars he found one bootprint and then another—it wasn't the man who had come into his and Jan's camp then. That one had been wearing moccasins and his foot was much smaller.

Justice flexed the fingers of his right hand, switched the Colt to that side, and walked on, moving slowly, listening and searching. But there was nothing to be seen, no one to be found. The man with the ax handle was long gone, leaving not a trace.

There wasn't much to do then but reholster the Colt and limp back up the alley to recover his hat. Wiping back his hair, Justice planted his slightly battered stetson and started on toward May Stansford's house.

He tramped up the wooden steps, noticing the charred clapboard on one side of the house. There were clean white curtains in the windows and a light burning behind them. There was a lion head clapper on the door and Ruff banged it twice.

"Just a minute."

The voice that responded sounded strong and cultured. A nice baritone voice that fit the woman who opened the door a minute later. She was fairly tall, around five-seven and somewhat heavy, fifty years old perhaps, with graying, tightly waved hair cut shorter than usual. She wore a gray dress with white lace at the neck and cuffs, and at that moment she was clutching a lace handkerchief in her white, age-spotted hand.

"Yes?" Her slightly demanding voice escaped from behind tightly spaced, small teeth.

"May Stansford?"

She studied Justice dubiously before answering. Ruff had a battered hat, a smudge on his face, his hair uncombed. His buckskins had seen travel, and getting knocked to the street back there hadn't helped them any.

She answered anyway. "Yes, I'm Mrs. Stansford. What can I do for you?"

"I'd like to come in," Justice said, looking beyond the woman to the blue-and-white interior of the house. It appeared slightly jumbled in a way Ruff couldn't immediately define.

"You'll have to tell me what this is about first," the lady said with a quick smile.

"It's about Clive Hickam's death. I'm a specially appointed army investigator. Ruffin T. Justice is my name."

"You . . ." The word reflected doubt that even the U.S. army would appoint a man like this to a position of responsibility. "Come in," she said taking a short, sharp breath, as if the invitation caused her some pain.

Ruff took off his hat and entered. The house was painted white inside, the furniture blue. The carpet had been torn up some and one wall showed signs of violence. There were a hell of a lot of books on a wall opposite and many others on the floor, stacked as if the woman had been trying to order them.

"I'm grateful that my house wasn't completely

destroyed by the renegades, but they made a terrible mess," May Stansford said as if sharing a confidence.

"Is there a place we can sit down?"

"In here." She led the way through an arched doorway to a small parlor where almost everything was intact. A huge bell-shaped glass lamp burned on an oval table.

Ruff sat down in a fragile-looking red chair, balanced his hat on his knee, and spoke to the woman across from him. "You knew Doctor Clive Hickam."

"I knew him as well as anyone in this town," she replied dryly. "No one in Clear Creek, or very few of us, could appreciate the doctor's mind. He was really quite brilliant, you know."

"So I've been told."

"By whom?"

"By his assistant, Jan Clark."

"That horrid person! Don't tell me she's here in Clear Creek."

Ruff frowned. "She's here. What makes you think she's a horrid person?"

"Certain things Clive told me about her . . . Well, never mind. You know her, apparently. What do you think of her?"

"I think," Justice said with a smile, "that she can be pretty horrid, but I don't think she's a bad person."

"If I told you what I know about her . . . But I shan't."

Ruff was stumped there. He didn't feel free to offer May Stansford the information that Jan was Dr. Hickman's illegitimate daughter. What in hell could Hickam have had against his own daughter?

"If it's something that might help me, Mrs. Stansford, I'd appreciate hearing it. I'm new to this investigating business, you see."

She didn't respond to his assumed humility or the

smile. "I'm sure it wouldn't help. The girl, after all, wasn't in Bismarck when Clive was murdered, was she?"

"No, she wasn't. Were you?"

The woman looked as if Ruff had slapped her. She stiffened and paled. "Obviously," she finally said. "All of us from Clear Creek were there, as I'm sure you know."

"At the dance, I mean?"

"Yes," she said, "I was at the dance."

Ruff changed tactics. "Have you any idea who could have wanted Hickam dead?"

"None." But she was lying. Ruff would have bet on that.

"I understand Doctor Hickam and you had a common interest in the local history. Did he ever talk to you about his work?"

"Did he? Of course he did; that was all we talked about. That, and literature and art. The Alpha Cave Civilization was virtually an obsession of Clive's."

"Did he ever take you out there?"

"Why ever would he?" the lady asked, and again Justice would have bet she was lying. "We enjoyed a pleasant intellectual relationship. He was virtually the only man in our poetry reading circle, the only one in our art group." She took a quick little breath and went on, "But we certainly didn't have the sort of relationship that would lead the doctor to invite me to go on a trip involving staying out for several nights in rough country, nor would I have accepted."

"I see. Is your husband dead, Mrs. Stansford?" Justice asked suddenly.

The woman did her stiffening routine again and glared at him as if from some great height. "What sort of question is that?"

"One not meant to be offensive," Ruff assured her.

"I just wondered. You've got a married woman's title, and yet I didn't get the impression you had a husband around."

"My husband's not dead, no. He's a teamster and he's gone a great deal. Just now he's working the freight line to Bismarck."

"All right. My main question, I suppose, is, do you know who might have wanted to kill Clive Hickam? So I'll ask it one more time."

"I have no idea. Many insignificant people around town may have disliked him, but I can't believe anyone wanted to murder him over whatever disagreements may have cropped up."

The lady was through talking. She made that clear by rising, folding her hands, lifting her head on its long neck inquisitively, and looking stonily at Justice.

"Guess I'll be going." Ruff stood and put his hat on. She had walked him to the door before Justice asked his one last question. "By the way," he said, "did Hickam ever show you any of that Spanish gold?"

"I don't know what you're talking about," the lady answered sharply, quickly. But she was lying yet again. Dammit all, she was lying, and Justice would have sworn an oath to that effect. He was more or less pushed out of the house to stand on the porch as she slammed the door and tugged the shades down. Taking a deep slow breath, rubbing his aching shoulder, Justice started back toward the hotel.

Thunder rumbled distantly and a flicker of lightning made a brief, sketchy tendril against the dark sky. Maybe Charlie MacDonald was a weather prophet, after all.

Ruff had already had enough of Clear Creek, enough of Jan Clark and this ancient Indian culture with its buried Spanish gold. There wasn't much he could do to back out of it, however; he would hold on, hold on until someone got hurt, until someone got killed.

And that would happen. If MacDonald could feel the approaching storm in his bones, then perhaps Justice was a prophet in his own right.

Because he could feel death coming. He could feel it breathing down his neck like the wind that had freshened and was now blowing cold off of the north.

7

Justice was in the hotel's cramped restaurant when Jan Clark made her appearance. She appeared smug and self-confident. She wore a green twill skirt divided for riding and a matching jacket, with a little Spanish-style black hat.

" 'Morning," Ruff said without much enthusiasm.

"Good morning, Mister Justice. Ready to leave?"

"Just about," Ruff acknowledged.

"We will reach the burial site today, won't we?" she wanted to know.

"With any luck. About nightfall. You still plan on staying down there despite what I've said?"

"Of course! I have work to do, a lot of work. And I won't be alone. You needn't worry now. I've hired on some men. Camp guards and scouts."

"You've . . ." Ruff didn't finish the sentence. It was then that the three men entered the dining room, and Justice knew. Charlie MacDonald still had his rain slicker on. It hadn't started raining yet, but it had rumbled and crackled most of the night. The storm was on its way in. The men stood three abreast in the doorway and Justice stared at them.

"What three men did you hire?" Justice asked wearily.

Jan watched his eyes and turned to see what he was looking at. "Why, these three. I'll introduce you."

"Don't bother," Justice said.

"I don't understand you. What's the matter now? You warned me against going down to Twin Buttes alone and now you seem angry because I've hired these men."

"I don't suppose there's any chance you know who those three men are."

"Of course I do—their names are MacDonald and the smaller man's name is Cannfield."

"They're outlaws, Jan," Justice said slowly, closing his eyes for a moment.

"I don't believe you," she answered sharply.

"Oh, you don't?" Justice's eyes had opened again.

"No, they warned me that you would say something against them, and they told me why."

Justice guessed, "Because I'm a womanizer."

"This is no time to be flippant. They told me all about you, Mister Justice."

"I've never met them before."

She insisted, "But they know your name, and when I told them I was with you, they told me some of the things you had done. Some of the—murders!"

"Sure, I'm a killer. That's why the army keeps me around on the payroll."

"I've also heard there are a lot of men on the run in the army out here," Jan continued. "They obviously aren't too particular about who works for them."

Ruff just nodded his head. "Whatever you want to believe, lady, but do yourself a favor—check around, find out who these men are."

"I haven't the time," she snapped. "I'm leaving this morning, now. Besides, if they're outlaws, why aren't they in jail?"

"I couldn't say," Justice answered, not believing any of this. "But that's where they belong."

"Nonsense!" She rose, her chair scraping the floor. "Besides, out here one man's as good as another. They're taking my pay, they aren't going to betray me while I'm giving them good wages."

"Hell, no! Not even for a cache of Spanish gold," Justice said acidly. "Look, lady, you're making a fool of yourself . . ." He took her hand and she spun away. Ruff kept his grip and came to his feet. The lady was furious. Kent MacDonald had come forward a step.

"Leave me alone," Jan Clark said, prying at his fingers. "I know what I'm doing."

"Sure. Your mind's made up, is it?"

Her eyes raked his face. Contempt turned her lips downward. "My mind is made up. You're a bully and a killer and I don't know what all. I trust those three men over you anytime."

"Maybe they're more suitable to what you have in mind." Recalling what May Stansford had told him, he asked her a few questions. "Do you have any idea why your father would talk against you? Did he hate you? Did he think you were a little too greedy?"

The seconds of silence that followed were heavy with hate and anger. "My father loved me," she hissed finally. "Now, let go of my arm. If you don't, I'll show you whether or not I can use this little pistol you made so much fun of. Even I couldn't miss at this range—and I'll kill you, Justice. I swear I'll kill you."

Justice nodded. His fingers opened and the woman spun away, tramping toward the door, where the MacDonalds waited, watching. Outside, thunder rumbled once again and a few heavy drops of rain pasted themselves to the dark window of the dining room. The faces that had been watching Justice and the girl turned toward the window.

Justice paid up and went out. He collected the gear in his room and paid his hotel bill. In a dark mood, he went out onto the plankwalk and watched as the rain began to fall over Clear Creek and the surrounding hills.

Putting on his own slicker, he tugged his hat down, hoisted his saddle and the Spencer, and started toward the stable. There was some activity there, although Ruff was glad to see that Jan Clark was already gone. She and her gang of hired killers. Justice couldn't get the idea out of his head that she knew exactly what sort of men they were. He hoped he was doing her an injustice.

Things hadn't been going real well, he reflected. Inside the stable he swung his saddle to the ground and stood waiting as the hostler finished helping a stocky man in a black town suit and hat.

It took Justice a minute, but he remembered who the man was. He was named Skye, Bert Skye, and he had run three saloons in Clear Creek in the days when there had been three saloons. He was a gambler and a pimp, and some said worse. He wore a diamond ring on his fat pinky and a diamond stickpin. He also wore a sleeve gun and was quick with the little, deadly toy.

"Howdy, Ruffin," the friendly, oddly broken voice from behind said.

Ruff turned, smiled, and stuck out his hand. August Delight was the one man in Clear Creek Justice could have been glad to see just then. The strapping, ruddy blacksmith had hands like hams and arms the size of some men's thighs, but he was a gentle giant: a former trapper whose voice had gone one winter when he was snowed in and half-frozen in the Big Horns.

"Hello, August, what're you doing out in the rain?"

"I'm out in the rain even when I'm inside now," Delight said. He went on, "Seen my house, have you?

69

Seen my barn? I've got no roof, Justice. I've got nothing but four hungry kids."

"Sorry, August."

"That's pretty much the way things go out here, isn't it?" August Delight asked with a shrug. He adjusted his suspenders, which bowed out over his massive chest and comfortable belly. "I've been near scalped, frozen, half-starved, burned out, and shot. But I never had Selma and the kids in those days. I can't rebuild just now." He tilted his head toward the man in the dark town suit; Bert was complaining that something was wrong with the saddle of the black horse the hostler was cinching up. "That's why I hired on as a guide for Bert Skye."

The blacksmith's face reflected momentary distaste, but August Delight wasn't capable of holding anger for long. A smile, accented by a broken front tooth, washed away that expression.

"What's Skye up to?" Ruff wanted to know.

"I don't know. Wants to go to Twin Buttes, that's all I know. Him and Doc Plimpton—know him?"

"I know him," Ruff said. Plimpton was a gunhand. One of the best they said, although that was all just talk, since no one had ever seen Plimpton work. He did his shooting alone, in secret, which was the reason he'd never been jailed. He was lean, almost emaciated. They said he had a bad liver, that he was dying, but Plimpton never let that slow him down.

"That's pretty bad company, August."

"That's not news, Ruffin. I didn't much want the job, but there's no one else wants to give a man work. I need to feed those kids. Bert Skye gave me sixty dollars in hard money to guide them, make up their camp, tend the horses, and hunt for them. I need the money. I'd work for the devil."

The big man removed his battered flop hat and

scratched at his thicket of straw-colored hair. "What in hell's going on down at the buttes, Ruffin? Why's everyone in such a damned hurry to get there—rain or storm or high water?"

"Trouble," Ruff Justice answered. "Trouble is what's going on there, August. If you can, pull out. If you can't, dammit, you watch yourself."

"Delight!" Bert Skye had turned toward them and now waved an impatient hand.

"Got to be going, Ruffin," August Delight said, taking Ruff's hand again. "I'll watch it. You do the same."

"Delight!"

August sauntered that way, big shoulders rolling. The gambler was in a hell of a hurry.

"He knows," Justice thought. He damn well knows that there's other men rushing toward the buttes.

"Pardon me," the man behind Justice said, and Ruff turned slowly, carefully. Something in the voice seemed to demand care.

Doc Plimpton was shivering from the chill of the rain. Pale eyes stared at Justice from out of a chalky, hollow-cheeked face. Plimpton looked like a man ready to step into the grave.

Or ready to put someone else there. He had his silver-mounted, walnut-handled Colt on his hip. Justice noticed the way the holster had been cut away, and the fact that the trigger guard had been sawed off the Colt.

"Going south, Doc?" Justice asked.

"Could be." Plimpton gave Justice a second look. "Ruff Justice, isn't it? Are you going south too?"

"Could be, Doc," Justice answered.

"Maybe we'll meet up down there," Doc Plimpton said, and his narrow, bloodless lips twitched into something that could be construed as a smile. Then, his eyes shifting slowly, seeming to look into all of the stable's dark corners, he nodded almost imperceptibly. He went past Justice toward Bert Skye, who was standing, reins to the black horse in hand, watching Justice from across the barn.

The three men swung aboard and rode out, leading a pack mule. August Delight lifted a hand and Ruff responded. The other two never glanced at him as they ducked their heads and rode out through the falling curtain of rainwater dripping from the eaves of the stable.

"Gettin' to be an interestin' little town, isn't it?" the hostler asked, mopping his face with a red bandanna. He blew his nose before tucking the bandanna away. "Glad all of those fellahs are gone, I'll tell you that."

"Got the dun for me?" Ruff asked.

"I've got him." The hostler's eyes showed momentary, remembered anger. He rolled back his shirt sleeve and showed Ruff a bandage. "He bit me. You told me he would and he did."

"Sorry about that."

"Christ, I've been horse-bit so many times I can't keep count—no apology necessary. Be glad to get that devil out of town too, though. No offense."

"No offense."

"Mind me asking where you're going?" the hostler said.

"South." Ruff's smile was grim.

"Not riding in those hombres' tracks, I hope. I like you, mister. I'd hate to hear something bad happened to you—and I can tell you one thing: anyone who goes off following the MacDonalds and Doc Plimpton both is going to be riding into trouble. Bad trouble."

Ruff had to agree, but there didn't seem to be much choice. He had been told to find Clive Hickam's murderer. He couldn't help but think that by following that bunch he would be riding in the right direction.

He swung aboard the dun, paid the hostler with two silver dollars, stared for a moment at the falling, cold rain, and then walked his horse out into the storm and onto the bad trail to Twin Buttes.

The storm had sputtered and faltered initially, but now it settled in heavily, darkening the sky, making shadowy sentinels of the trees, and causing the distant rolling plains to appear like a vast sea.

Ruff had followed the trail southward for most of an hour, but now, far from the town, he swung away from the road and rode up into the oak-clad hills. There was no sense in making it too easy for an ambusher.

He didn't exactly expect to be ambushed, but he knew the character of the men he was back-trailing and there was no point in taking a chance.

The rain hammered down, streaming off his hat brim, hissing through the trees. A thousand tiny rivulets formed in the hollows and gulleys and began rushing toward the flats where the river called Clear Creek ran toward the distant Heart River.

The thought that ran through Justice's mind constantly was that this was a hell of a lot of activity. Considering the fact that there had only been a single gold coin found—two, counting the one the unknown gunman in Bismarck had carried. What was the total value of those coins? A hundred dollars or so at a guess, and yet seven people were risking their resources and possibly their lives on that hope.

Was there more gold? Clive Hickam had had all the time in the world to poke around the Twin Buttes cave site and the two coins were apparently all he had come up with. Unless there was a cache of some kind that only Jan Clark could find, maybe one that he had secretly written to her about.

Thinking about the woman scientist with the lush, beautiful body and the hard, harsh manners caused

Ruff's jaw to clench slightly. Was she angry, scared, or just tough?

Lightning crashed against the sky, lighting the sky briefly with pale, living creatures that disappeared almost as soon as the eye could fix on them.

The rain fell and now the storm had really settled in, a constant, dark, and brooding thing that sighed and groaned with the effort of it all.

Justice forded a creek and guided the dun up a grassy slope. A stunted pine waved frantic arms at the wind like a sorcerer determined to fend off the forces of the storm. Ruff then crested a rocky knoll to overlook the dark distances ahead.

And just for a moment he saw him. A figure, small and scuttling, as quick and transient as the figures etched by lightning against the shifting sky.

Ruff heeled the dun sharply and the horse broke into a run. Ruff unsheathed his Spencer just in case, tucking the beaded elkskin scabbard under one thigh.

There had been someone there, running downslope, weaving through the oaks, but damn all, he was gone again! Vanished into the night and the storm.

Ruff took the time to swing down, searching back and forth across the slope for sign. He found it and knew it.

Moccasin tracks, but moccasins such as he had never seen until a few days ago. They weren't Sioux or Cheyenne or Crow. But the intruder who had come into Ruff's camp back there had also worn them.

The man, whoever he was, was following them, or following Jan Clark—following anyone who might be riding to the burial site.

"Who are you?" Ruff Justice asked. "What are you?"

The cold wind blowing into his face gave no response. The rain fell constantly and the day grew darker. Ruff swung aboard the dun again, still wondering. Whoever this one was, he was silent and quick, knowing the land and how a man can use it to his advantage. It couldn't be, but somehow Justice had the feeling he was being tracked by a ghost, the ghost of a people long gone. The last of the ancient ones.

8

Night fell early. Justice was camped in the pines above the roaring gorge. The water rolled and boiled, showing white in the darkness, and thundered southward to meet the Heart. Justice had no fire and would have none on this night. In the distance, however, he could see the wavering red cone of someone's campfire. It appeared and disappeared eerily behind the shifting clouds, now moving low across the earth. A mile or two farther on, Justice could at times make out the two crumbling monoliths known as Twin Buttes.

It was there that Clive Hickam's dreams had lived. The dream of finding proof for his theory that Father Aguilar had trekked from Mexico into this wilderness and found an aboriginal culture. It was there, if anywhere, that the secret of Hickam's death would be found.

Wearing his slicker, his hat pulled low, Ruff Justice crouched against the cold earth and stared out through the pines and the rain. He didn't like the feel of this one, not a bit. "Thanks, Colonel," he said to the night, and the wind in the trees seemed to chuckle back infuriatingly.

Then, so distant that it might have been a waking dream, there was the pained groaning of a man. It came not from the camp below, but seemed to come from the buttes themselves. Ruff had heard only one other sound like that, and he frowned deeply.

It sounded for all the world like the death song of an Indian, the prayer of a man preparing himself for his last battle.

The Cheyenne came in the night.

Justice was in his blanket, sitting propped against a tree when he saw them by a sudden jagged spur of lightning. Ten men, perhaps more, slowly winding their way through the hills, moving south and west.

Justice glanced quickly toward the campfire below him, but the rain had put it out. The Cheyenne wouldn't find them tonight, except by pure chance. Morning would be a different story.

Stone Eyes was back.

Justice watched the Indians' progress until he could see them no more, trying to gauge their speed and line of travel. When they were gone, he was no wiser than he had been. They seemed to be meandering aimlessly through the hills, but it couldn't have been aimless. A war party doesn't drift through the rain and the darkness for no good reason.

Were they looking for an enemy, then? An escaped prisoner? A meeting ground? There was no telling, and it didn't matter. Whatever their original purpose was, they would certainly kill any whites they found in their path, as a matter of course.

And the whites seemed to be right in their path.

Ruff rose and saddled his horse. It was two hours before dawn, but he wasn't going to be doing any more sleeping that night.

Dawn was gray and silent. The rain had stopped but clouds hung heavily above the damp hills and grassy valleys. Ruff rode on toward Twin Buttes, not knowing what sort of reception to expect. He had every legal right to be there, but what did the MacDonalds know about legality?

Ruff tracked them in easily: three riders moving with surprising haste, Jan Clark's wagon leading the way, and having a tough time of it over the uneven ground on this side of the river.

He saw nothing of the other party. Bert Skye was perhaps lying low, watching to see what was going on. It was even possible he had ridden on through the night to reach Twin Buttes first. And what did they think they were going to do when they got there? Tear the mountains down looking for a small cache of gold that might not even exist?

"Maybe I'm the one who doesn't know what's happening," Justice said to the dun, which twitched an ear and turned its head as if to bite. Ruff slapped the muzzle away. "Maybe there is gold and it's out of the ground and these folks know exactly where."

Justice reached the little valley that funneled through the pine-clad hills and opened up onto the Heart River. He found the Clark camp near the base of one of the great buttes and rode in openly.

Cannfield, looking disgruntled and tired, was unloading the lady scientist's wagon. Jan Clark, who had been unpacking something, straightened up and wiped at her forehead with her wrist. She recognized Justice at a distance and Ruff saw her entire body stiffen with rejection and disgust.

He splashed across a narrow feeder creek, its bottom littered with round stones that were nearly all the same hen's-egg size, and rode into the camp. There was no sign of the MacDonald brothers.

" 'Morning, Miss Clark," he said.

"Get out of here."

"Thought I'd see if there was any coffee around." Ruff began to swing down, seeing the lady step back, seeing Cannfield start toward him, smiling. Cannfield smelled work that he liked better than unloading wagons.

"The lady said you're not wanted, mister," Cannfield said. He put a hand on Scalawag's bridle and the horse nipped at his ear. He leapt away yowling. Justice just watched him.

"No fire?" Ruff looked around, seeing signs of work now—old work. A half-dozen pits had been dug in the clay bench, all of them about five feet square, roped off with a single strand of cord. "I was really hoping for coffee. Cold, isn't it?"

Cannfield had braced himself. Jan Clark, seeing the expression on the young outlaw's face, had started backing away. She was hunched forward slightly, her eyes wide behind her spectacles. The wind molded the white blouse she wore to her breasts nicely, but there was no time to enjoy that.

"I want you out of here," Cannfield said. "Now!" His voice was a hiss like a snake's; his eyes had a snake's jewellike gleam. His hand was near his holstered pistol.

"I assume you're talking to me," Ruff Justice said. He was stroking Scalawag's muzzle.

"You know damn well I am."

"Going to kill me?" Ruff asked the frustrated kid. Cannfield was used to being taken seriously, very seriously. When the MacDonalds rode into a town, everyone knew it. Men moved out of their way when they swaggered up a street. Just now Cannfield was alone, without his cold-blooded cousins to side with him, and he wasn't quite sure how to proceed—except to start shooting.

The tall man in buckskins had ice-blue eyes. He had a tanned lean face—a face that was unscarred but that looked as if it had seen war, and plenty of it. He didn't back down an inch as Cannfield took a step closer.

"Damn you," Cannfield said, "move out or I'll kill you. You know who I am?"

"It might surprise you," Ruff Justice said quietly, "but I don't give a damn who you are. You're a kid with a gun who wants to shoot me, that's all that matters."

Cannfield couldn't figure it. He was losing his confidence quickly. In a moment he was going to lose it all. He snarled something scarcely human, and his pride caused him to make a mistake: he reached for his pistol and snapped it upward.

Ruff Justice kicked out with his long leg and his boot heel smashed into Cannfield's face. The kid staggered backward, his gun dangling from limp fingers, his face a mask of hot blood from his broken nose.

Justice had his own Colt out now, just in case, but he wasn't going to need it. Cannfield went to the ground on his back and stayed there, moaning, holding his face. Ruff walked to him and kicked the pistol away.

"Coffee?" he asked Jan Clark, and the scientist hurled herself at him, showing her teeth. Violent intentions lined her lovely face. Ruff caught her by the front of her blouse and turned her, using one foot to trip her so that she fell and sat down hard on the damp earth.

It began to rain once more.

Jan Clark said, "You hurt that boy. Broke his nose."

"Hard to understand, isn't it? Just because he wanted to kill me. Lady, you should have been a judge."

"He was just trying to frighten you off, to do the job I hired him for."

"Is that what he was doing? It looked like murder to

me," Justice said. He looked skyward. "Got shelter anywhere? It looks like it's really going to come down for a while."

"The caves," she said. Her chest was heaving, her eyes furious, but it seemed she had given up on trying to get through to the tall man. That was fair; Ruff had certainly given up on trying to reach the lady.

Justice stuck out a hand and yanked her to her feet. She ended up just a few inches from him, her lips parted in anger or in some other emotion she wasn't able to define for herself. She remained there a moment too long, and Justice smiled.

"I hate you," she said. But it was a soft comment somehow, as if confusion was seeping into her emotional vocabulary. Ruff let her go, helped Cannfield to his feet, and started toward the cave.

Cannfield was groggy enough at first not to know who was steadying him as he walked rubber-legged toward the shelter. When he figured it out, he shook free of Justice's arm—and promptly fell down.

"Come on, tough guy," Justice said, pulling him up again.

Glowering, Cannfield let himself be taken to the cave.

Inside, the cave was lighted by a dully glowing oil lamp. A table had been dragged in and set up. The lady scientist's books, papers, and a few small tools provided decoration.

"Got any adhesive tape?" Ruff asked. "Better pack that nose and tape it."

"My cousins'll kill you when they get back," Cannfield growled.

"Nice way to talk to a man who's going to patch you up," Ruff Justice replied.

"You're insane," Cannfield shouted, his voice breaking into a near shriek. "A crazy man!"

"Sure. Got tape, Jan?"

"Doctor Clark," she said automatically.

"And cotton. This might hurt a little, Cannfield, but you don't want a crooked nose to mar those pretty features of yours, do you?"

Cannfield didn't answer. In another minute he couldn't. Justice packed the cotton into his nostrils and the kid passed out cold. Ruff laid him down on a blanket-covered cot Jan Clark showed him and finished the job.

"It'll do. Never set more than three or four noses, but this one wasn't broken bad," Ruff said.

"Good. Send me your medical bill. For now, why don't you leave?"

"Not yet. I want to look around."

"You're interfering with my work."

"You're interfering with mine, lady. Where are the MacDonald brothers, anyway?"

She smirked. "So you are worried about them, after all."

"Worried *for* them if they run into some of the people who are out there."

"What do you mean?" Jan Clark asked, looking toward the mouth of the cave, through the rain to the river that rushed past the buttes.

"Cheyenne are back. At least a small war party. Not far from here either."

"You're making this up."

"Sure."

When she spoke again her voice sounded dry. "What would they want here?"

"There's no telling at all. If they know about these caves—and I assume they do—they might want to take shelter here until the storm passes."

"Now I know you're just trying to scare me," Jan

Clark said, but her voice was little more than a squeak.

"Where'd the MacDonalds go?"

"Hunting meat. They should be back anytime. You'd better leave. They'll—"

"Kill me? Those nice boys."

"Justice, I might have made a mistake about the three of them," Jan Clark said, and it was as close as she could come to admitting that she could ever make a mistake. "I heard them talking last night. About various things . . . some of it wasn't very savory."

"All right. We're stuck with them now, though." Jan heard the pronoun and looked at him strangely. "Yes, I'm staying. I want to look around a little too."

"For the gold." She removed her spectacles, polished them, and tucked them away in her skirt pocket. She damned near looked female.

"I don't think it's here, Jan. If it is, I don't really care. I'd just put it away in a bank and worry about it. I'm here for one reason: to find out who killed Clive Hickam. Your father. If you care about that, then you won't mind me staying for a time."

"What can you find out here?" She spread bewildered arms.

"I don't know. Maybe nothing, but this is where it all began, isn't it?"

And maybe where it ended. Jan Clark was still looking out of the cave and now she gave a tight gasp. She put her glasses on and told Justice.

"They're coming. The MacDonalds are coming."

And damned if they weren't.

9

•••◦——◆——◦•••

Both of them wore black rain slickers now as their horses splashed across the river ford. Kent MacDonald had a gutted buck mule deer across his horse's withers. Their faces were grim as they approached the camp and Charlie unlimbered his rifle when he spotted Justice's dun pony.

They walked their horses into camp. Kent unloaded the deer with one arm, and they rode right up to the mouth of the cave before swinging down, each holding a Winchester loosely.

Their eyes went first to Cannfield, who was lying on the cot, face taped. Then they shifted to Justice and stayed there.

"What happened?" Charlie MacDonald asked in a voice that might have once been southern but now had the burr of the plains in it.

"He tried to kill a stranger," Justice said. His voice was casual, soft. He didn't want trouble here and now. Meanwhile his thumb was hooked in his gun belt, his hand not far from the Colt. Charlie MacDonald noticed it.

"You?" MacDonald asked.

"That's right."

"You gunned him?"

"That wouldn't have been right—not for a simple mistake in judgment. I kicked him."

"You're a thoughtful man," Charlie MacDonald said carefully.

"I try."

"What the hell is he doing here?" Kent MacDonald demanded belligerently.

Jan answered him. "Mister Justice is here because he's an expert on local Indians and the government thought he might be able to help me sort things out here. He'll know which artifacts and carvings are Sioux or Cheyenne and not Alpha Civilization." She spoke rapidly, throwing in the word "government" many times as if it were a talisman against which the MacDonalds couldn't strike.

The MacDonalds didn't believe that was the real reason, but they were willing to let it drop for the time being. Maybe the word "government" had dissuaded them; Justice thought it might have had something to do with the Colt riding on his hip.

"Didn't see any sign of a Cheyenne war party, did you?" Justice asked.

That one did shock the MacDonalds a little. They glanced at each other with concern. "Cheyenne? Around here?"

"I saw them last night. Stone Eyes maybe. You shouldn't have shot that deer: it'll bring them running." Ruff's eyes were steady and cold. "I wouldn't do any shooting around here for a while."

Charlie MacDonald's eyes went again to his cousin, who was having some trouble breathing now. "No," MacDonald said, "we won't do any shooting—now."

Jan Clark spoke rapidly as relief untangled inside her and became a wild garrulousness. "Very well, then, if you men will see to dressing the deer and starting a fire so that we can cook it, Charlie, maybe you'd better haul some water up as well; the rain is coming down, but it looks like it might get worse. No more digging outside tonight. Oh, Kent, maybe you'll bring in my shovel and screen as well."

Ruff stood watching the MacDonalds. They had uncoiled a little, but like rattlers, they still bore watching.

Jan Clark touched his arm. "You can come with me, Mister Justice."

"Where?" Ruff asked without looking at her.

"I want to go up into the caves. I have Clive's maps—we certainly can't work outside." A nervous little titter followed.

"All right." Justice took his first real look around the cave as the MacDonalds, silent and menacing, left them and went out into the rain.

The cave was nearly square except for its vaulted ceiling. It showed signs of natural erosion where the river had formerly cut away at the soft sandstone; it showed signs of human effort as well. One wall was smoked by ancient fires and a few scratches, petroglyphs that could no longer be made out.

"I don't think you much need my help to tell you which artifacts are Sioux and fairly recent and which belonged to the cave dwellers," Ruff said.

"You know I don't," Jan Clark said, recovering some of her haughtiness. "I just told them that so they'd leave you alone."

"I appreciate that. You could have turned me over to them—seing as you hate me so much," Ruff said. She was about to respond seriously, but Justice couldn't help breaking into a grin and her mouth clamped itself shut into its habitual straight line.

"Do you want to look around with me or not?" the scientist demanded.

"Sure. Let's have at it."

"If you'll get that lantern—not the one on the wall. Right there. I'll get Clive's chart."

"You still can't call him father," Ruff Justice observed.

"A man who plants his seed somewhere and goes away with never a second thought is hardly a father."

"How do you know he never gave you a second thought? What did he tell you?"

"Well"—she made a gesture of dismissal—"what would you expect *him* to say?"

"Can't decide if you love him or hate him, can you?" Ruff asked.

Surprisingly Jan took that one unemotionally and considered it. "I guess I can't," she said at last. She stood with the chart in hand, looking almost childish. "Are you ready?"

Ruff looked toward the cave mouth, seeing the MacDonalds in conference. "Yes, I'm ready." He told Jan, "You know they're just waiting around to see if you can find the gold for them. They know you've got the charts and whatever else you're not sharing. They know it's beyond them to find the gold."

"I'm aware of that now. The gold, however, is not my primary concern."

"No?" Ruff smiled again, and the woman turned sharply away from him, leading off into the depths of the cavern where once—maybe—an ancient people had lived and had greeted a priest from the far south. Greeted him and honored him? Or murdered him?

They found a doorway carved into the sandstone wall of the cave. Rubble had fallen down and had been pushed to one side by Clive Hickam. Once, the entrance had been entirely concealed by stone and earth. Now it led into a long, upward-slanting, narrow corridor.

Ruff could easily touch both walls as he walked,

holding the lantern for Jan Clark, who worked her way cautiously, preceded by her long, wavering shadow.

"How far does this go?" Justice asked.

"This corridor is only a few hundred feet long, but it opens onto several rooms. There are other passageways leading off these. Clive explored approximately a third of the rooms—living chambers he called them, though I suppose that's speculation, since he didn't have any evidence that any Indian or aboriginal actually lived in the rooms."

"Don't suppose this was all some sort of temple, do you?" Justice asked off the top of his head.

"That would be speculation too, Justice. And I'm not given to such exercises in imagination."

"No," Ruff said under his breath, "you wouldn't be."

A series of rough steps, uneven in width and height, took them to a low dark room. As Justice entered, the lamp sprayed orange-gold light into the corners, revealing nothing but another empty chamber.

"Nothing for bedding," Ruff said. "No straw—rats would have dragged that off, though. No poles."

Jan Clark looked at him as if he had just succeeded in explaining the obvious to a blind woman. "This way," she instructed.

"Just a minute," Ruff Justice said. He was watching the corridor intently.

"What is it?"

"I thought I heard something, someone moving back there."

Jan tried to remain calm, but she trembled a little. "The MacDonalds?" she suggested.

"Maybe. I don't think they're going to come following us, though. They'll wait until the gold, if there is any, is dragged out for them."

"Who, then?"

"I don't know," Ruff said. But he had an idea.

"It's ridiculous, no one could be there except the MacDonalds. There's no other way into the cavern."

"That we know of," Justice commented.

"I have the map right here." She slapped it against her thigh as if to support her argument.

"Yes. A map of a third of the caves—isn't that what you said? A third." Ruff looked upward and then shook his head. He couldn't quite believe it himself, but it was possible there was someone else in the mountain.

"Just gravel and sand falling somewhere," Jan Clark said. But she didn't believe herself entirely either. "Let's continue on."

A second corridor, narrower and taller, led upward from the room. Someone had done a lot of work—years of it—in carving out this warren. Perhaps to protect his tribe from enemies the way a prairie dog cuts a labyrinth of tunnels in the earth? It seemed possible.

"What about the other butte?" Justice asked as they entered the corridor and began picking their way over rubble. "Are there any caves in it?"

"None that Clive discovered," the lady answered.

"The gold coin—where did he find that?"

She turned and looked at him. "You'll see. Up ahead."

"Is there any way to get to the top of the butte?"

"Not that Clive ever found, although logically you'd think the Indians—if we can call them Indians—would have needed a way up. They could have had crops and possibly a redoubt up there in case of an attack—especially in later years, if it is true that the nomadic tribes drove them out or killed them."

They rounded a sharp bend in the corridor and saw the floor of the tunnel level out. Directly ahead of them was a wall of stone.

"Here," Jan said, and her voice was very small. "This is where the coin was found."

"You'd think he'd have gone ahead through the wall here," Justice remarked.

"Yes, but this was the first piece of evidence that he was right about his theory. It was more important to Clive to report his findings. Then, too, the Cheyenne had nearly arrived by that time and he had to get out of the area."

"Someone must have warned him," Ruff noted. "He wouldn't have seen Stone Eyes for himself—and lived."

"That's right, I suppose," Jan Clark said. Her eyes showed incomprehension. "So what?"

"Who was it? Who warned him?"

"I don't know. What difference does that make?" she asked.

"Whoever it was knew where Clive Hickam was, knew what he was doing, and probably knew what he had found. He would have been bubbling over with the need to tell someone."

"You're reaching, Justice, looking for an easy answer to your problem."

"Mine? You don't care who killed your father?" The lantern chose that moment to flicker out and they were left in almost absolute darkness. The wick sparked dully, but aside from that, there was nothing at all, no light in the world, only the cold, enclosing walls of the cavern.

"What happened?" Jan asked in a hollow voice that echoed through the cavern.

Ruff shook the lantern. The fuel splashed in the reservoir reassuringly. "I wasn't watching the wick. Burned down, I guess."

"Well, turn it up, for heaven's sake. Light it and let's go on."

"In a minute," Justice answered.

"Then I'll . . ." She reached for the lantern, but in the darkness her hand fell on Justice's forearm and it lingered there for a minute, squeezing his arm. Ruff put his arm around her waist and she didn't move. He could hear her rapid breathing, and as he drew her nearer he could feel the rise and fall of her breasts against him. He bent his mouth to hers and kissed her once, hard, feeling her lips part, feeling the surge of physical interest in her body.

Then she drew away so sharply that she almost fell. Her voice was little more than a gasp. "Please light that wick."

"Sure."

She saw him strike a match and she stood trembling, no doubt fearing that she would see that smile on his lips, but there was nothing of the sort there. He lit the lantern and it flared to life, casting a halo around them.

"Now," Ruff Justice said, "we can go on."

"I don't know if we can go on this way," Jan said, putting her palm against the wall of fallen stone in front of them. "It might take hours, days, or even months to get through. It might be nothing at all. A dead end beyond the stone." Her voice was unsteady and she spoke rapidly, touching her lips once with her fingers nervously.

Ruff Justice noticed that, and he noticed something else. He showed it to Jan Clark.

"I think we'd better try to go through here," Ruff said. His finger was still resting on the small emblem he had found, carved into the wall high up so as to be nearly unnoticeable. Inscribed by primitive hands, it was quite clearly a cross.

"God," Jan whispered. "Can that be a coincidence?"

"Maybe. But I've been around some. I've seen

swastikas and sunbursts and thunderbirds—but an Indian or a pre-Indian carving of a cross, never."

"Then . . ."

"Then," Ruff Justice finished, "maybe there's a reason for this stone having been put here. It didn't collapse naturally. Maybe, just maybe, you've found something Clive Hickam missed in his excitement, or maybe he was interrupted before he could find it. Maybe you've found the way to the remains of Father Aguilar and his expedition."

"And," Jan Clark said, "to the rest of the Spanish gold."

Ruff couldn't define her tone of voice. Hopeful, lost, greedy, fearful, it seemed to make the darkness come alive with ancient ghosts.

"Let's hope not," he said finally. "It will only mean the beginning of trouble. The MacDonalds are down there. And the others."

"What others?" Jan asked in much the same tone.

Ruff didn't answer. It wouldn't do her any good to know about Bert Skye and his hired gunfighter. Justice looked at the wall of stone, wondering.

Behind it was some secret—something living still, though it belonged to the past. The bones of a Spanish priest, the shimmering remnants of a golden treasure . . . or the ghosts of a vanished, tormented people. He had no urge to tear down the wall, to find what lay behind it, but it had to be done.

"Now," Jan Clark said, her head tilting oddly forward, her fingers clutching as if at some unseen golden goal. "Let's take it down now."

10

They agreed that it wouldn't be a good idea to return for a pick and shovel or a sledge. Justice and Jan Clark got to it with bare hands, removing stones from the top of the wall, knowing full well that a tribe of people could have blocked the shaft for hundreds of feet.

The question in Ruff's mind was, Why had they built it at all? Had it been to form a burial cairn, to keep the foreign spirit of the priest and his alien god away from the people, or to hide a treasure?

"There could be nothing at all here," Ruff said more than once. "This doesn't have anything at all to do with Aguilar or his gold."

But even Justice didn't believe it. He couldn't convince himself that the Indians, the cave dwellers, the whatever-they-were, had piled this rock here for no purpose. They worked on in the semidarkness, the lantern making eerie shadows of their moving bodies against the walls and ceiling of the cave.

"Is there enough fuel in the lantern?" Jan asked.

"I hope so."

The woman's face was smudged, her hair had come unpinned. She had taken her glasses off to protect them as she worked and her stern features seemed younger and hungrier, almost earthy.

"I feel something," Jan said. She scrambled over the rock, touching Justice on the shoulder. "Can't you feel it?"

"No. What do you mean?"

"Air. Right here. Air seeping in from above."

She was right. It was moving air, and it carried a scent of its own. Ancient, yet fresh. Jan was tearing at the rocks now. Her right hand had blood on it. Ruff tried to slow her down but it was no use, and he found himself working as fast as she was after a while, enlarging the hole.

The breeze was very definite now. Jan's face glowed in the lantern light and it was taut, intense—maybe just a little greedy.

"Look out," Jan said. She had pulled one log-shaped rock free and let it roll down to the cavern floor behind them. As if it had been a sort of keystone, other rocks followed, bounding and sliding downward.

When the dust cleared, they had a hole big enough to crawl through. Jan looked at Ruff, her hand stretched out to him.

"The lantern," she said breathlessly.

"Want me to go through first?"

"No! I want to see. I want to know . . ."

"Take it easy. It could be nothing," Justice reminded her.

"I know it is something. I can feel it, can't you?" the lady asked.

As a matter of fact, he could. He could feel *something*. Something that stung his nostrils, lifted his heartbeat, crept slowly up his spine like cold fingers.

He gave Jan the lantern and watched as she wriggled through the opening in the wall of stone. When her feet had vanished, Justice went after her.

He crawled up and over the rocks and followed the glow of the lantern into another section of tunnel, not much different than the one they had just left. High ceiling, narrow walls, rough dark floor.

There was no gold there, no hidden temple. Jan's face sagged. "We didn't gain a thing, not a thing," she said. Her shoulders were hunched with disappointment.

"Sure we did," Justice said, putting a hand on her shoulder. "We can go on now, can't we?"

"Go on where? We're off the chart now."

"Let's see. Any coal oil left in that lantern? I don't want to go back in darkness."

Jan just stood there, bathed in her own frustration. Justice took the lamp from her unprotesting hand and shook it.

"There's enough for a while. Let's have a look. That breeze is coming from somewhere."

He had shifted the lantern to his other hand when a stray beam of light caught the bright golden eye staring back at him from the floor of the cave.

"That what you're looking for?" Ruff Justice asked.

"What . . . another coin!" She got to hands and knees and it was more of a religious act than the act of a scientist trying to examine the find. Her fingers, smeared with drying blood, picked up the gold piece and turned it over. She turned to Justice with something like reverence in her eyes. "Another one. Clive was right. He was right!"

"It looks like it. Let's move on."

The woman got reluctantly to her feet and followed as Justice moved along the corridor, which now twisted upward and left. Justice found the second marker and showed it to the lady scientist.

"Another cross."

"Father Aguilar *was* here."

"Maybe. It looks like it. Why the crosses, though?" Justice asked.

"To mark the way?"

"The Indians would have known the way, Jan."

"Then perhaps the priest carved them himself. To mark the way to where he left his gold. He became sick, perhaps—all of his expedition did. He sent word back to the authorities in Mexico telling them where he was, but it never got there." Maybe Jan Clark should have been the one writing the dime novels, Ruff thought, and not the colonel. Then again, she might be right.

She went on, "These crosses were left to guide the searchers to the gold, don't you see?"

Ruff only nodded. He was getting a little short of breath, despite the breeze that blew toward them with more intensity.

Jan Clark panted a little herself. Carried away with her own unscientific tale, she had found the conclusion. "The Spaniards might have carried something that made them all fall ill. Smallpox, say. And that could have been, must have been transmitted to the Indians. That's what happened to the cave dwellers—not warfare with the Sioux, not drought or earthquake."

Justice was half-listening and then he wasn't listening at all. They had reached a new level, a place where the tunnel widened and flattened and led into a vast chamber.

The rocks lining the wall were oddly shaped. Justice lifted his lantern and drew nearer. Then he muttered a slow, soft curse. Now he could tell what he was looking at—they weren't rocks at all.

"My God!" Jan Clark cried, putting her hands to her lips. She took an involuntary step backward as if to retreat from the reality of what they were seeing.

The walls were lined with them, in hollows cut into the solid stone. The dead lay mummified, staring at eternity. Ruff Justice went closer, Jan Clark just behind him as if drawn along on an invisible wire.

"The cave dwellers," she said with a touch of awe.

"Looks like it."

They weren't Spaniards. They wore the remains of crudely woven fiber blankets wrapped around their waxed and leathery bodies. A lost century lay before their eyes.

It wasn't easy to tell what they had looked like in life, but there wasn't much of the true Indian about them. They had very high foreheads and seemingly small noses. Their lips were very full. One man, a chief or honored elder still showed the signs of a tattoo.

Jan Clark stared at the parchmentlike flesh and the primitive clothing. "Carved into the stone," she noted. "Symbols of some sort. That's a snake. Their names, perhaps? Or their totem?"

"Hard to tell. Maybe you can work it out. Look at this one."

Ruff showed her the cross carved into the wall. It wasn't the same as the others; it was large and ornate. The dead woman who lay beneath it must have been a convert.

They moved on, finding another chamber filled with row upon row of the dead, finding the mouth of another upward-slanting tunnel.

"Another cross," Ruff pointed out, but Jan Clark had found something that excited her more. She held up the heavy, crumbling object.

"Armor. Spanish armor, Justice. A breastplate. It's corroded, but that is what it is. He was here, Clive was right. My father was right!"

Three steps into the new tunnel they found an even greater treasure. Ruff saw it in its carved niche, waiting patiently for the future to discover it.

"What is it, Justice?" She gripped his arm tightly as Ruff removed the wood-bound book from the alcove. There was a cross carved into the rotting wooden cover. The yellow parchment inside, unevenly trimmed and loosely bound, was alive with Spanish words.

"It looks like we've come up with Father Aguilar's diary," Justice said.

"Let me see. Can you read Spanish?"

"Some, not this brand. I can make out the words but not the flow of things."

"Hold the lantern up then." Her voice and hands were both trembling as she opened the diary. "I'll see if I can't read it . . .

Anno Domini 1542, by the grace of God and of the Virgin, I Father Jesús Ortega Aguilar, on a mission of conversion among the heathen people in the new land do with a party of eleven soldiers and four Indian guides begin my excursion into the lands of the far north where it is said the savages who have never heard of our good Christ are among the fiercest in the world . . .

"Justice!" Jan's eyes lifted from the page. They glowed with excitement. "This is it. This is what my father was looking for. This is his vindication. He was right. Everything he insisted upon was right."

"Looks like it," Justice said. His own voice was subdued. Jan Clark didn't understand and he didn't choose to explain it just then.

He didn't want to tell her that they weren't alone inside this mausoleum.

The footprint was clear in the stone dust of the corridor, and it wasn't something left by the ancient ones or their ghosts. It was a moccasin track such as Justice had never seen until a few days ago. The track of the man who had followed them—or another like him. It proved one thing: the burial site wasn't as deserted as they believed. Someone was still living there. A living, breathing man. A cave dweller.

"We'd better get on back," Ruff said.

"No! We have to go on. First let me read the diary, Justice, and then—"

"We'll run out of oil for the lamp."

"Well, how much is left?" She reached for the lantern, but Ruff pulled it away. Then she saw it in his eyes and she cocked her head. "What's wrong, Ruff?"

"I don't want to run out of fuel for the lamp."

"You're not telling me something. We have to go on now. We haven't found the end of the trail the markers indicate. You know as well as I do that if there is a treasure, we have every chance of finding it now."

"There'll be another time," Justice said.

Jan still couldn't puzzle him out. She knew he was holding something back, but what? "With the MacDonalds following us?" she asked. "Once they see the diary, they'll know—and I won't leave the diary, not now."

Ruff might have argued with her but suddenly there was a real reason to go on instead of going back. The shots sounded from below, distant echoing, pinging things hardly like the report of a weapon—but Justice had heard guns before.

Both of them turned, staring down the tunnel.

"What?" Jan asked.

"Trouble. Come on. Let's move it."

The shots continued, sounding like rocks falling down a well. They were pathetic imitations of gunfire, but up close they were causing death.

They moved on hurriedly. Upward. If there were more crosses carved into the walls, they never saw them. There wasn't time to look, to investigate. There was death back there somewhere.

The breeze continued to freshen. Now it smelled like rain and open country. The trail Jan and Ruff were following dead-ended abruptly. They found themselves in a small, vaulted cul-de-sac. Above, gray light shone dimly through a nearly round opening partially covered by brush.

"The top of the butte," Jan said.

"Looks like it." Justice handed the lantern to Jan. "Put this out and hold it."

"What are you going to do?"

"Get out of here," Justice said, looking upward.

His first attempt missed badly as the rock crumbled in his hands and he fell roughly back to earth. Setting himself again, Justice leapt up, found purchase, and drew himself up into another world.

The top of the butte was covered with sage and sumac; scattered oaks and pines grew there. The sky was gray with cold drizzling rain. The distant lands were bleak and empty.

"Ruff?" Jan Clark called.

He peered into the cave and stretched out a hand. "Come on up."

The lady looked around in a lost way, tucked the diary inside her blouse, tossed the lantern up, and then leapt for Justice's hand.

He caught her, tugged her up, and together they sat on the damp earth, watching the rain and catching their breath. They still heard distant shots, although these were spaced farther apart now.

Ruff got to his feet. "Where are you going?" Jan Clark asked. She looked small and uncertain now. The wind had tousled her dark hair, the rain had dampened it.

"To see what's happening," Justice said.

"I'm going."

"No, you're not. Sit there for a minute," Justice ordered.

She stared at him blankly from behind misted glasses.

Ruff moved off toward the rim of the butte, checking his Colt over as he moved. In sight of the rim he went to his belly and inched slowly forward. From the edge of the caprock he was able to look down at the river, the base camp, and the trees.

What he saw was enough to make him swallow a curse and clench his jaw. They had trouble—worse trouble than he had expected.

The Cheyenne had come.

11

---◆---

Looking past the rain-swollen, gray-and-white river to the pines clustered near the shore, Ruff Justice saw the Indian warriors. They were painted and bare-chested, continuing their holy war, Stone Eyes' jihad against the whites. They had counted coup on this day—a man's body lay sprawled against the rocky beach before the cave entrance. Jan Clark's wagon was on fire, curling black smoke into the gray skies. Goods were scattered across the ground.

"What's happened?" Jan was beside him, on her feet, peering down through the rain at the scene below. Her mouth opened and she started to say something more or perhaps cry out.

Ruff Justice yanked her harshly to the ground. "Shut up, woman! I told you to stay back there, didn't I?"

"But . . . I didn't know!"

"Now you do. Be quiet. They're liable to find us anyway, but let's not make it any easier for them."

There wasn't anything at all they could do just then but watch—watch the Indians as they prepared to make camp, watch the rain and the occasional lightning, watch the dead man sprawled on the beach below.

Cannfield was never going to get over that broken nose. That was who it was—the odd white smear on his face had eluded Justice until he figured out that it was the adhesive tape he had put there himself. Where the other two MacDonalds were, alive or dead, he had no idea.

"Let's pull back," Ruff said at last. "They don't seem to know anyone else is around—at least they don't know where."

"But how will we ever get off here?" Jan asked.

It was a good question. Trapped atop the butte without food or shelter, and without any blankets they could do nothing about their situation. Nothing but hope the renegade war party would drift away. But they seemed to have no such inclination.

"Wait them out," Ruff said.

"The army will be coming, won't they?"

"The army," he had to tell her, "seems convinced that Stone Eyes is gone for good."

But the colonel had been mistaken there. What was this small war party doing here, if not waiting for Stone Eyes himself and his renegade army? If the Cheyenne were trekking south once more, Clear Creek itself was in their path. It had already been burned and besieged once, and had apparently survived to be reborn another day. Now, unknowingly, it might be living out its last days. Someone had to get through to warn the town—someone, but Justice saw no way to make it there himself.

Maybe there wasn't even a way to survive.

They withdrew to a jumble of gray granite boulders sheltered by a tangle of live oaks. The rain still slanted down, but inside the thicket of trees, the wind was cut by the massive, split rocks and it was relatively dry, relatively warm.

Ruff sat staring out at the stormy day. It was

unlikely that the Indians would come looking for them, unlikely that they could tell there were any more whites around, but you never knew. The tunnel might draw their curiosity, and the tunnel led to the top of the butte and Ruff Justice.

The lady sat reading her diary. From time to time she would look up at Justice, her finger poised on the page as if she were going to read him a passage. But she kept silent, reading the ancient priest's saga of a long and dangerous journey through an unknown land.

It began to grow dark and the storm decided to finish the day with a thump and a bluster and a roar. Rain washed down out of a black sky, causing the trees to shudder and moan.

"Justice."

The voice was small and unfamiliar. Ruff turned his head and looked at Jan Clark, who had her glasses off, placed beside the priest's diary. Her white blouse was wet and it clung to her breasts, clearly showing her taut pink nipples. Her hair was loose, longer than Ruff recalled.

"What is it?" Ruff asked, his voice barely carrying above the whistle and hiss of the wind.

"Cold. I'm cold, Mister Justice, and wet and we might die up here."

"We won't die," Justice said.

"No? You guarantee that?" Jan Clark smiled faintly. "Come sit with me. Come be with me. They can't find us in the darkness, can they?"

Ruff rose and walked to her. He stood over her for a moment, staring down at the lady scientist, the lost little girl. He put his hand on her head and rested it there. She was looking up at him still, her green eyes dark and liquid in the night. Her hand took his and moved it lower, placing it over her breast. Her heart was thudding like a hammer.

"Come down to me," she said as if she had trouble speaking. "I don't want to die, Justice."

Ruff got to his knees, taking her face between his palms. She watched him, her lip trembling, her mouth slowly opening, her eyes closing. Justice kissed her, kissed her until he took her breath away and she was left with a trembling that had nothing to do with the chill of the night.

He slowly unbuttoned her blouse and she automatically pulled away, but he pressed his lips to her uncovered breasts and she drew his head to her, giving a little sigh as she lay back, her arm across her face, her dark hair spread out against the grass.

Ruff's hand went to the waistband of her skirt, finding the two wooden buttons there. He slipped the skirt off and stood to undress. It was cool but Ruff felt little of it. In another minute, as he pressed his flesh against Jan's, he felt it not at all.

Ruff took her hand and guided it downward, placing it on his shaft. She let her fingers encircle it, feeling it swell and lengthen with a sort of awe and fear and intense interest mingled. She took her forearm from across her face and looked into Ruff's eyes, smiling once as she began to stroke it reflexively.

"I've never felt anything like that," she said.

"No?" Ruff kissed her ear.

"Does it feel good?"

"Yes, it does," he said, kissing her throat.

"What else feels good?" she asked, her voice childlike again, shy and yet eager.

"Want me to show you, Jan?"

"Show me everything, Justice. This might be my last night."

"Or your first."

He slipped a finger between Jan's warm smooth thighs, finding her cleft damp and ready. Slowly she spread her legs, watching his face all the while, looking for approval.

"You're a beautiful woman, Jan."

"How can you say that?"

"It's true." Ruff shifted himself and let Jan touch the head of his shaft to her body. She trembled again but continued to guide him in, to gaze at him with wonder as he slid into her body, flooding her with heat and unsuspected need.

Her searching hand found his sack and cupped it as she arched her back and her hips found the timeless rhythm, driving her pelvis against his. She half-sat up suddenly and bit at Ruff's bare shoulder, clinging to him.

"God, Justice, it's good."

"Is it?" he asked with a smile. His own body had begun to answer her rhythm methodically, stroking and lifting her. "How good is it?"

She couldn't answer. She bit at her finger as her body responded to Ruff's question with a rush of fluid. Jan's head rolled from side to side, her body writhing beneath his.

"Never . . ." she said. "Never knew," and Ruff drove deeper into her. His hands roamed her breasts, slid down her back to her buttocks, clenching them tightly. Lifting her higher, he got to his knees and drove it home time and again, his own need rising, his loins aching as Jan Clark wriggled and panted, clutching at him. Finally with a moan that was smothered by distant thunder, she reached a body-racking climax.

"You," she panted. "Now you." And her fingers groped for his shaft, stroking it as Ruff penetrated her body, urging him toward a hard completion. She felt him swell and find his release, felt the throbbing of his body and the rush of his climax, and the lady scientist, exhausted, lay back on the grass as lightning carved the sky with light.

Ruff lay against her, kissing neck and shoulders, smooth pale breasts, touching his lips to her ears and eyes, wondering. Wondering why May Stansford had said that Clive Hickam hated his daughter, wondering what it really was that had brought her to Dakota—the lure of gold, was it? He wondered why she had hired the MacDonalds. Was that out of hurt pride and ignorance, or did she have another motive?

She was beautiful, young, complicated. Ruff's instincts told him that she was all right, a lost child still looking for her father—trying to please him, trying to find her womanhood, which she had smothered with intellectualism or out of resentment toward her father.

Still he wondered. He lay awake a long time, wondering about Jan Clark.

Until some time after midnight when a trick of the wind, a gap in the bluster of the howling storm let the voices drift to his ears and Ruff rolled from his makeshift bed—they were no longer alone on top of the butte.

"What was that?" Jan sat up, her eyes wide, hair tangled by lovemaking.

Justice put his finger to her lips. "Get dressed," he said into her ear.

She didn't question him anymore or argue. She was well aware of their situation. She looked questions at Ruff as she dressed, but Justice couldn't answer them. He didn't know who was out there, how many there were or what they wanted.

If they were Indians, they might well have found their footprints. There was nothing to do but have a look. And if they were Stone Eyes' warriors, a single shot would bring more of them storming to the top of the butte—more braves who wanted scalps and blood.

"I'm going to have a look-see," Ruff said casually.

Jan wasn't fooled by his tone of voice. "Indians," she said almost soundlessly.

"Maybe." His smile didn't do anything to allay her fears. "Still have that little popgun of yours?"

Jan fingered the pearl-handled .32 in its holster and nodded mutely.

"Keep it close," Justice said. Then he bent, kissed her, and was gone into the night. Thunder rumbled again and lightning crashed against the earth. Ruff Justice moved in a crouch through the live oaks, following the path they had used earlier. The storm was very low. Clouds rushed past Justice; driving winds snapped the fringes on his buckskins and drifted his long hair.

In his hand the big bowie was cool and damp and solid.

Justice went to his belly. There were three of them there and suddenly: night demons, Cheyenne, heavily armed. The wind shifted the feathers knotted into their long hair as their painted faces lifted, listening, searching.

They had found Ruff's sign.

The rain hadn't been enough to wash it away, and now they were following it upslope toward the rocks where Jan Clark waited with her puny pistol. Waited for the death she had been certain would find her on this night.

One of the Indians crouched and fingered a track, and Ruff heard him say, "One man . . ." The wind carried away whatever else he might have said.

Justice waited, his teeth clamped together, the bowie in his hand. Three of them, all armed with feathered, brass-studded Winchesters. It wasn't going to work. Yet, if he opened up with the Colt, he was going to call the rest of the war party to him.

There just wasn't any choice, however. There was nowhere to run. There was no way down off the butte—certainly no way Ruff Justice was going to find in the darkness of the howling storm.

And if he didn't stop them now, they were going to find Jan. If he could take one of them, possibly two, Jan might have a chance. A very small chance.

For Justice himself it was going to end here—he knew it with sudden certainty. Well, he had lived long and hard. He had fought duels down on the bayous, his wrist strapped to big Jack McGee. Fought with pistols with a French nobleman, hunted the renegade Cheyenne Iron Heart and lived, taken a white woman from under the eyes of Elk Stick, traveled to San Francisco and to Europe with Bill Cody and his show, cleaned up a town on a bet with Hickok . . . a lot of times, a lot of places, a lot of memories, most of them good.

Ruff never thought he could last forever, not living the way he had. But he wasn't quite ready for it to end. The renegade Cheyennes drew nearer. Two of them jogged forward, eyes lifted to the knoll, and Justice knew that they had sensed that was the hiding place of the whites.

The third man lingered for some reason. Lingered briefly over the footprint, his face a puzzled frown. Perhaps he had seen those particular tracks before. But he had done too much thinking, gotten himself too far behind the others, and as he passed Justice's hiding place, the man in buckskins rose from the earth, his bowie slashing out as his hand clamped over the Indian's mouth.

Cold steel sliced through flesh and arteries and trachea, and the Indian brave went to the ground, strangling on his own blood as Justice stepped back.

The others had continued to jog and now Justice broke into a dog trot, following them toward the rocks and oaks.

Lightning struck close, filling the air with the scent of sulfur and lighting the landscape with white-hot intensity.

The Indian turned at the wrong time.

Looking back for his fellow warrior, perhaps; or hearing Justice's footsteps somehow above the storm, the warrior spotted Ruff and shouted something, his finger pointing out the onrushing white.

The first Cheyenne brave lifted his rifle to his shoulder and Justice had no choice. He drew his revolver and fired twice, the bullets ripping through the renegade's chest, slamming him backward, his howl of pain lifting above the sounds of the storm, echoing across the butte. The second Indian dived for the ground, rolled, and came up sitting. His Winchester repeater spat flame at Justice, the bullet whipping past the scout's head.

The Colt spoke twice more with authority. Ruff's first bullet nearly lifted the top of the Indian's head off; the second stopped his heart.

Justice was reloading on the run, and when the other man raised up from the ground, Ruff still had the loading gate open, fumbling with a .44–40 cartridge. He swung his Colt that way, but the man threw his hands high.

It was no Indian Justice had thrown down on. Nor was he white. He was small and as dark as a black man, his hair straight and sawn off, his hands holding a double curved bow such as Ruff had never seen—and half a dozen twisted arrows.

Ruff's Colt never wavered. He had an idea who he

was facing, but it seemed incredible. The last one. The last of the cave dwellers, the last Alpha man.

The squat dark man moved to the bodies of the dead Cheyenne renegades and squatted down. Then, unexpectedly, he smashed their faces with his fists. Standing, he grinned and said something in a language that sounded more like grunts and whistles than human speech, and held his hand high as if in triumph.

Behind Justice other voices sounded—Cheyenne voices—and he wheeled that way. More of Stone Eyes' people were coming to investigate the source of the shots. It was all up now.

The cave man said something and beckoned in a way that was apparently common to all civilizations. He waved his hand, looked at Justice, and started on tentatively. Ruff had nothing to lose. He followed the little man in skins.

The little man jogged a way and Ruff followed him through the storm. They were nearly at the rocks where Jan hid, and Ruff started to call out to the cave dweller to slow him up. But he seemed to know, and he veered toward the rocks, slowing to let Justice catch up with him.

They found Jan with the tiny pistol in both hands, muzzle raised, her rain damp face tense and frightened.

"Let's go," Ruff Justice said.

"Where?"

"I don't know. All I know is we can't stay here. They're coming. Stone Eyes' warriors."

"But . . ." Then she saw the man, the thing beside Ruff, and her mouth opened in a soundless cry. "Who is that, what is he?"

"The man you came to find, Jan. The last of his kind. We're going with him."

"You trust him?" she asked in astonishment.

"It doesn't matter much if I do or don't—he's the only chance we have, Jan, the only chance of survival."

She nodded, suddenly decisive, grabbed the priest's diary, and came to Justice, holstering her little pistol. From the mouth of the tunnel they heard Cheyenne war cries, and the little man with them gestured excitedly. It was time to go, but where they were going and what lay at the end of it eluded Justice. The little man couldn't speak any tongue Ruff knew, nor could Justice understand the cave dweller.

But the man was their only hope. The Indians were coming on the run and the three of them ran on through the crash and rumbling of the storm. Jan looked at Ruff Justice as they ran, but there was nothing he could say. There was no explanation possible. They ran on in blind trust, following the ghost of an ancient civilization through the thunder of the night storm.

12

·····———◇———·····

The rain drove down. The war whoops behind them were carried by the wind. Ruff ran on, his breathing ragged now. Jan stumbled and he yanked her upright. They had placed their lives in the hands of the small dark man with the twisted arrows who jogged effortlessly ahead of them.

And if he was treacherous or simply mad, they would die on this night.

They were nearly at the edge of the bluff. Ruff could see the rain-swollen river below, running white and fast across the land.

"What's he expect us to do? Climb down," Jan shouted.

"I don't know. Keep running."

"I can't," she called back, but then the cave dweller stopped, his bare chest rising and falling. He looked at Ruff, grinned crookedly, and showed them exactly where they were going.

He squatted and pulled at a patch of sagebrush, and as Justice watched, the brush tilted up as if it were a hinged trapdoor. The cave dweller pointed down and Ruff looked at Jan.

"What do we do?" she asked.

"Go down or stand here and face the Indians," was Ruff's taut reply.

The cave dweller was motioning frantically and Ruff helped Jan into the hole. The little man had gone back a way and was erasing their tracks with sagebrush switches. Given time, the rain would finish the job so that the Cheyenne would find that their quarry had simply vanished into thin air. Their bet then would be that the whites had gone over the edge of the crumbling butte.

Ruff followed Jan into the hole, dropped six feet to the floor of a small chamber, and stood waiting for their guide. They didn't have to wait long. Quick and agile as a monkey, the cave dweller dropped into the hole beside them. He stopped to raise his arms and shift back the flat rock that was the hole's cover, and shut out the dim light of the world outside.

"The lantern," Ruff said.

Jan produced it, and in the darkness Ruff struck a match, touching it to the wick. Their guide grinned with delight, showing brown teeth, and led them hurriedly down a short down-slanting corridor to a second chamber.

"What's he doing now?" Jan asked.

Ruff could just shake his head, watching as the little man clambered onto a benchlike rock and thrust his head up. The head vanished and Justice smiled. He had a second hole to peer out of, and from this he was now watching the renegades. After a minute the cave man leapt down to stand hunched before them.

He showed Ruff a tattoo on the back of his hand. Charcoal had been rubbed into knife cuts. The shape was that of a cross.

"What's he telling us?" Jan asked, but Justice had no answer for her. The little man was still grinning and now he said something that sounded like Tata.

Jan said, "Is that his name?"

"I don't know. It'll do. Tata," he said to the little man, and the last of the cave dwellers jumped up and down with glee.

The man who was called Tata then showed Ruff something scratched into the rock wall of the cavern. They were human figures and there were dozens of them. They wore war bonnets and were dismembered. Unexpectedly a clenched fist went up and the little man hit the carvings as he had hit the dead Sioux on the butte.

"What's he doing? What's that mean?"

"His enemies," Ruff told her. "Men he has killed. The Sioux are his enemies; so, it seems, are the Cheyenne."

Jan just stared at the carvings. When had Tata become an enemy of the Sioux? Had they always been his people's enemies? Had they killed his family, his friends, all of the Alpha people? Tata couldn't tell them.

He started away, waving a dark hand, and Ruff and Jan went on. They followed a winding corridor more crudely made than those they had been in, one hardly wide enough for a man to move through.

"Where's he taking us?" Jan gripped Ruff's arm. The lantern cast eerie shadows on the walls of the cave and made Tata appear like a gnomish demon.

"No idea. Away from the Cheyenne anyway."

Away and downward, still downward as the tunnel narrowed still more and steepened. Ruff had to duck now to clear the ceiling.

"How much fuel is left in that thing?" he asked Jan Clark.

"Darned little," she said, shaking it.

"Keep the wick low."

"He must have fire, torches," she said, nodding toward Tata.

"Does he? Maybe so. It's obvious he knows his way around here without needing light. Maybe he has none."

"I can't breathe," she said, and it was true that the air was getting thin—thin and heavy with rock dust. "Why don't we stop and rest."

"He's not tired. He figures we're not, I guess."

The lantern, turned so low that the wick barely burned, cast a dim, flat beam of light against the walls of the cavern. They had reached a second room, this one larger, too large for a single man to have carved in a lifetime. It had to have been made by the tribe in the days when the Alpha people flourished.

Tata was grinning as he turned. In the corner were his gifts for these strangers, whites who presumably knew how to use them and would value them.

Ruff saw the cave dweller crouch and pick up a breastplate: Spanish armor, not corroded as the one Jan had discovered was, but gleaming dully in the lamplight, carefully maintained and polished over the centuries. He offered it to Ruff Justice.

"What does he want?" Jan asked.

"It seems he wants me to put it on," Ruff answered dryly. "To prepare for battle maybe."

There was a helmet and halberd as well. These Tata placed at Ruff's feet, still grinning. Once again, his grin fading, he showed them the tattooed cross on his hand.

"I don't know what's going on in his mind," Ruff Justice said. "Maybe he thinks we're Spaniards come back."

"He's lived alone, Ruffin. For a very long time—in the darkness of the cave some of the time."

"I know it." It was a place to tangle old legends and

116

fears with reality. Tata, a man alone, had perhaps appointed himself to watch these articles for the day when a Spaniard would return to battle, to chase the enemy away again, glittering and clanking on horseback in armor—maybe that was what had happened once before. Tata couldn't tell them.

Ruff gestured to the little man to place the armor back in its corner. Tata looked disappointed, but only briefly so. When he stood again, his eyes were lighted with an idea that glowed brightly. He picked up his bow and his twisted arrows and started off again, calling Ruff and Jan after him.

They went down a narrow corridor to a second room, a room where water seeped in and glossed the cavern walls, where bats clustered by the thousands on the high ceiling. Something hissed and grumbled deep in the cavern, beneath its floor: an underground branch of the river, perhaps.

"Ruff!" Jan took his arm again and then Justice saw it too. Another cross carved into the wall. Tata grinned, nodded, and led them forward.

In the next room they found the priest.

Mummified, prepared for burial in the manner of the cave dwellers, he had a bible in his hands, a moldering, decaying thing. He wore a long black robe and sandals. His face in death was ascetic, powerful, his nose large and sharp, his forehead high. His head had been shaven.

Tata got to his knees and crossed himself, the last of a dead people saying his confession to the dead priest who had traveled so far to save souls and had lost all of his living converts to disease or war or time.

Tata rose, temporarily solemn. Then he grinned again and led them on.

"What now?" Jan asked, still unsettled by the priest's body. She didn't have to wait long for an answer. The lantern had begun to flicker and dim, but it cast enough light for them to see the cache of gold.

It rested in three small leather trunks, gleaming softly, a vast fortune untarnished by the ages. Jan stopped and stared as if frozen, touched by a golden sorcerer's hand. Tata grinned happily. He had finally found something that pleased his visitors.

Justice stood and gazed at the gold as well, but his mouth was tight. There it was, the golden treasure men had died for. More would die, Justice thought. More would scheme and betray and murder for it.

"We could leave it here," Justice said.

"Do what?" Jan spun on him, and for a moment her face was as fierce and savage as one of Stone Eyes' renegades'. "Oh, I see. But, Justice, don't you realize what that gold could mean?"

"Blood."

"The means to proceed with the work here, to discover all about the Alpha civilization, to learn about Tata and his people, the means to educate and explore and publish findings. It can't be left." She shook her head. "No, Justice, it just can't be left here."

The voice of Charlie MacDonald said, "And I vote with the woman, Justice. What do you think of that?"

Justice whirled, but it was too late. The MacDonald brothers, their rifles ready, had him covered. Tata leapt for the entrance to a tunnel mouth, but Kent MacDonald hammered him down with his rifle stock, leaving the cave dweller unconscious, sprawled on the cavern floor.

Kent cocked his rifle but Charlie called out, "Not in here, you idiot. Kick those arrows away and leave him be." MacDonald touched his sandy mustache and smiled. "But don't think that means I won't shoot you, Justice, if I have to. Why don't you shuck that gun

118

belt? Do it now, before something bad happens to you, will you?"

Ruff didn't have a lot of choice. He unstrapped his gun belt and tossed it to MacDonald.

"How did you find us?" Jan asked. "How *could* you?"

"Nothing much to it," Charlie MacDonald said, turning his head to spit. He touched his pale mustache again. "We were doing some camp work when the Indians come. They come chargin' across the river, firing from horseback. Hell, it was lucky for them they hit a damn thing. Unlucky for Jody Cannfield. The kid lost his head as usual and tried for his horse. Cheyenne got him.

"Me and Kent made for the cave. Didn't know where we was goin', but figured they'd play hell gettin' us out of there while we had our guns. Indians spread out lookin' for us and we come in deeper. Sometime back we heard voices—you'd be surprised how far sound carries in those caves. It was you and Justice talkin', so we come ahead. Here we are." Charlie MacDonald looked at the gold and smiled. "And glad we come."

Kent MacDonald had lost his black rain slicker somewhere. He hadn't lost his savage expression. "Want me to cut this little fellah's throat, Charlie?"

"Don't be stupid," Charlie MacDonald said. "What the hell is he anyway?" he asked Jan. "He's no Cheyenne, that's for damn sure."

"He is a cave dweller," Jan Clark said. She had fished out her spectacles, cleaned them, and put them on. She looked a little more self-assured that way. "One of the aboriginal inhabitants of these caves. A living anachronism."

"How's that?" MacDonald asked.

"He can't be replaced. His scientific value is incalculable," Jan added.

"Valuable, is he? We got him, who's gonna buy him?" Kent asked.

"No one would *buy* him. He's a human being," Jan Clark responded.

"Then he ain't worth much, is he?"

"Worth something to us," Charlie MacDonald said.

"What do you mean, Charlie?"

"Just this: if anyone knows a way out of the butte without running into the Indians, it's the little man there—assuming he ever wakes up again. Didn't crack his skull, did you?"

"I don't know." Kent tipped back his hat. "Didn't intend to."

Justice had been silent. He stood near the gold watching MacDonald with ice-blue eyes.

Charlie MacDonald seemed a little unnerved by Ruff's gaze. "What are you looking at, scout? What are you thinking?" he asked.

"Thinking you're playing this wrong, Charlie," Ruff Justice answered. "You'll never get out of here at all if you plan to take the gold."

"You know damn well I plan to take it."

"How much do you think those three trunks weigh? Do you have any idea?"

"I've hefted some gold in my time," Charlie MacDonald said with a smirk.

Tata was stirring on the floor and for a moment they all glanced that way.

"Without horses you're just not going to make it anywhere," Ruff Justice pointed out.

"We'll make it—or you'll die trying. You're carrying that gold, Justice. You and the . . . whatever the hell he is. That monkey there."

"With the Cheyenne in pursuit?"

"However it has to be done. If you think I'm leaving that gold, you're crazy."

"I'm wondering if you're not crazy anyway."

Charlie MacDonald didn't like that. He disliked it enough to step forward and clip Justice above the ear with his rifle barrel. Justice spun away, clutching at his ear, which trickled blood. His head was ringing. Jan Clark screamed and Charlie MacDonald grabbed her by the arm and shook her violently.

"You shut up, lady," he hissed. "You just shut up or I'll kill you, I swear it. You bring the Cheyenne down on us and you'll go first." He shook her again, harder still. "You understand!"

"I understand," Jan managed to say weakly.

"Now," MacDonald said, stepping back, "one of you tell that monkey to get us the hell out of here."

"Just how are we supposed to do that? He doesn't speak Cheyenne, English, or Spanish or Sioux," Justice pointed out.

"You figure it out. Just get us out of here—and now. The renegades can't be all that far behind."

Ruff didn't feel much better than Tata looked when he bent down beside the cave dweller. Tata's hair was heavy with blood, matting his thick black hair. He looked fearfully—or was that anger?—at the Mac-Donalds. Ruff smiled and crouched. Blood still trickled from the scout's ear. The little man cringed as Ruff squatted beside him, and that hurt Justice more than the MacDonalds ever could.

"We have to go," Justice said quietly. "*Salir disparados*. The Cheyenne are coming." There was no response. Justice tried speaking in the Sioux tongue, but Tata's face showed no greater comprehension. Finally he resorted to sign language, pointing at the MacDonalds and the gold, at Jan and himself. "We

121

have to go. The Indians are coming," Justice said, and Tata nodded. He got to his feet, Ruff rising with him.

Tata touched the blood on his own head, the blood on Ruff's face, and glanced at the MacDonalds, seeming to understand at last. He wiped back his hair and nodded again, saying something in his odd whistling tongue.

"We're going?" Kent MacDonald asked.

"Looks like it," Charlie said. "You, Justice, take that chest—the big one. Give the monkey the other. Lighten up the third trunk a little. Lady Bifocals is carrying that."

"She can't lug that thing," Justice objected.

"She will. Or she stays. I don't give a damn either way," MacDonald said.

"I'll make it, Ruffin," Jan Clark said. Her lips barely moved as she spoke. "Don't worry about me."

Ruff shifted the gold a little, placing more coins in his trunk. Tata reached in and placed some more in his own, apparently understanding what was going on. The trunk the outlaws expected Jan to carry must have still weighed around sixty pounds. That didn't seem to bother the MacDonalds a bit. Ruff strapped his trunk shut, bent his knees, and shouldered his burden.

"Jan . . ."

"Darn it, Justice, I said I'll make it."

And she got it up, somehow. The MacDonald brothers watched her lift it, staggering under the weight. Only Justice saw what Tata did then. His bow and arrows lay scattered on the ground, but the cave dweller managed to find one twisted arrow, which he slipped inside the leg of his hide trousers.

Tata looked at Justice, fearing betrayal, but Ruff gave the man a broad wink. Surprised, Tata gawked and finally winked back.

"What the hell's going on here?" Charlie Mac-Donald asked.

"Nothing," Ruff answered.

"Then let's move. Goddammit, can't you hear the Cheyenne coming?"

And Ruff Justice could. Back in some unseen corridor the sounds of softly moving, moccasinned feet was audible, and the outlaws moved their prisoners out. They were loaded down with the treasure the ages had delivered to them, the lost gold of the ancient Spaniards who had come to conquer and convert and who had lost not their souls but their lives.

They had died here, in this lonely, honeycombed butte. Ruff Justice didn't expect his own fate to be much different.

"Move it," MacDonald said again, and even the hard-bitten outlaw looked frightened. Stone Eyes was coming, bringing war death with him.

13

They followed Tata by the light of the dying lantern. Justice was the second man in line, the trunk cutting into flesh and bone and slowing him to a hobbling, staggering pace.

Behind Justice was Kent MacDonald. The outlaw prodded Justice constantly with his gun barrel. It didn't do a damn thing to speed Ruff up. With a hundred pounds of gold on his back he wasn't going anywhere in a hurry.

Behind Kent was Jan, her labored breathing loud in the close confines. Charlie MacDonald came last. His slicker swished and crackled as he moved.

Behind them somewhere, farther back, were the Cheyenne, stalking still, looking for blood.

"Does the monkey know where he's going or not, dammit?" Kent MacDonald growled.

"He knows," his brother answered.

"Maybe he does. Maybe he's not going to show us. Maybe he's going to leave us in here."

"Shut up."

"I don't like this crap, don't like the dark, Charlie."

"You don't have to like it—just keep moving. Justice, dammit, hurry up!"

Ruff asked over his shoulder, "Do *you* want to carry it?"

"Smart-ass bastard." Kent MacDonald, who was sweating now, obviously growing claustrophobic, lifted his rifle as if to club Justice down with it.

"Put it down, Kent," Charlie MacDonald thundered. "We need him to carry that gold."

"Yeah, for now we need him," Kent said, wiping at his face, which was dripping perspiration.

"For now."

"Later I'll have the bastard."

"Later," Charlie MacDonald said, "you'll be welcome to him."

Tata had paused as if confused, but Justice doubted that he was—maybe he was thinking of the woman, trying to give her a rest.

"What'd he stop for? What's going on? I think I hear Indians. Can you hear them, Charlie?" Kent MacDonald was slowly going to pieces.

"Look, you idiot, there's three tunnels. Maybe he don't know the way."

But Tata looked at Justice, who nodded and started on, taking the left-hand tunnel.

It was an endless hour later when Justice smelled water in the air and heard the rush of the river. A star appeared out of nowhere, framed in a blue-black oval ahead of them.

"The river," Kent MacDonald said with vast relief.

His brother snarled at him. "Shut up! We don't know who's outside."

No, they didn't know that. It could be Stone Eyes himself with a hundred warriors. They edged nearer to the cave mouth. They were twenty feet or so above the waterline. A tree bobbed past on the storm-corrugated surface of the river. The clouds showed gaps of clear, starlit sky now, but the wind had grown stronger, howling as it touched the cavern mouth with a warning.

"Have a look, Kent," Charlie MacDonald said.

His brother looked at him doubtfully, nodded, cocked his Winchester, and peered out cautiously. He was half-smiling when he looked back.

"Seems clear. Don't mean they're not there, but I can't see 'em. We're around the far side of the butte. Can't make out the camp."

"All right." Charlie made up his mind. "We go down. Quick and quiet. Justice, you're first."

"Thanks," Ruff said. "Making a target of me?"

"Get, or I'll shoot you myself."

That sounded doubtful, but Justice figured it was best to do what Charlie wanted. Besides, he had no desire to stay in that damnable cavern any longer—not with the Cheyenne in it somewhere.

Ruff looked at Jan, offered her a smile, and lowered his heavy trunk to the ground. Moving out, he dragged the gold with him down the muddy, dark bank to the river, where he concealed himself in a clump of willow brush, looking upstream and down. Kent was right: just because they didn't see the Indians yet didn't mean they weren't out there.

He heard a small scuttling sound and looked back to see Tata making his way down the bank. The little man no longer grinned. He came up beside Ruff, remaining crouched himself, his alert eyes searching the shadows.

Jan came next. It was a rough trip down the slope as she slipped and then skidded, losing hold of the trunk, which tumbled toward the thicket of brush. Ruff crawled out, dragged the trunk into concealment, and watched as Jan scampered to them.

The outlaws followed. The clouds parted for a brief moment, fully illuminating their movements, and

Justice winced, praying that Stone Eyes didn't have a sentry on this side of the butte.

He turned his eyes to the butte briefly. It loomed above them, massive, stolid and dark, still holding its secrets. Centuries had passed inside its tunnels and vaults. Only Tata knew what had happened there, or a part of it. Tata, who had been brought out forcefully into the modern world. What would happen to the little man now?

Thinking of Tata brought Ruff to a new sequence of conjecture. Tata had been out on the plains. He had looked into their wagon one night, then followed them back to the butte. Had Tata also followed Clive Hickam to Bismarck? Had he killed him with a twisted arrow for desecrating a burial site?

It was hard to believe. Tata had been only friendly and open with Ruff and Jan. Or perhaps he had just been biding his time. He had seen the thunder of Ruff's Colt.

"All right," Charlie MacDonald said after a full minute. "Let's move out. We've got to cross the river someplace; let's try it here."

"There's a lot of current," Kent said, "and no ford."

"There's a lot of current everywhere after the rain. The only ford I know of is up at the main camp. Want to go back there, Kent?"

It was a taunt and Kent started to respond but fell silent. It was obvious who the lead wolf was. Charlie MacDonald pushed Ruff's shoulder.

"Go on, scout, we'll cover you."

"Terrific," Justice muttered. All they wanted him to do now was cross a rain-swollen river on foot, while carrying a hundred pounds of gold, in full view of any watcher on the far bank.

"Move it," MacDonald said, and Justice got to his feet, shouldering the gold, which buckled his knees a little. He shook his head and started out, moving through the willows in as much of a crouch as he could manage, carrying the trunk.

The water was white and rapid when Justice eased into it. At thigh depth it threatened to sweep him away. It rushed cold and teasing past his body. His boots sunk into the mud with each step, the added weight making progress ridiculously slow and tedious.

Fortunately the river didn't get much deeper. A bar underfoot led most of the way to the far beach and Justice, half-expecting to take an Indian bullet before he reached it, finally clambered from the river. Exhausted, he dropped the trunk and sat on the beach, half-concealed by pine trees, taking in slow, heavy breaths.

He could see Tata laboring across the river, following Ruff's route.

If they sent Jan next . . . Justice looked around. Drop the gold and head for the hills. Work their way up the ridge and cut a track for Clear Creek. The MacDonalds could carry their own damn gold if they wanted it.

Charlie MacDonald was a bastard, a bully and a killer—but he was no fool. Kent MacDonald came next, holding his rifle high, and only when Kent had Ruff and Tata under his sights did Jan Clark start across.

Jan had taken a dozen steps when she went down, arms flailing, the trunk falling into the river.

Ruff was on his feet, but Kent MacDonald said, "Just sit down again. She'll get up."

She did, clumsily, gasping for air. Her bifocals were gone, but she managed to fish around and find the trunk, heft it, and carry it to the shore. She flopped down on her back beside Justice, holding her abdomen as her chest rose and fell. Kent MacDonald had his eyes riveted on her blouse, which was pasted to her breasts.

"You all right?" Ruff asked.

"I don't know. Is this the way you live? Is it always like this out here?"

"Pretty much."

"I'm going east," she panted. "Far east. As soon as I can go."

"They can't let you go, Jan," Justice told her as gently as he could.

The girl sat up suddenly, studying Justice with those eyes that seemed so wide without her glasses.

Charlie MacDonald was wading toward them, his dark slicker's tails floating on the river.

"What do you mean?" she asked.

"Think about it. They want the gold, only the gold. I don't know if it rightly belongs to you or to Tata or the government of Spain, but it damn sure doesn't belong to the MacDonalds."

"I don't care if they take the darn gold."

"I don't either. Let them take it and be damned, but they won't see things that way."

Charlie was ashore now, moving heavily toward them in his waterlogged clothes. "Get up, get moving, dammit! I'm not sittin' here waiting to see who shows up."

"We need horses, Charlie," Kent MacDonald complained.

"I know that, dammit! What d'ya want me to do? Take 'em from the Indians? Get up, get walkin'. Triple C isn't too far off. Maybe Sam Cribbs has still got some horses."

Cribbs? The name sounded familiar to Justice, and he was puzzled until he recalled that the Triple C was where Jenny Farnsworth's friend Susan lived.

"If he knows Stone Eyes is here, he's run for Clear Creek. If he had time," Kent said.

"You got all kinds of objections just now, Kent. You give me a better idea and we'll use it."

Kent offered none.

Justice helped Jan to her feet and shouldered his trunk. It was going to be a long cold hike.

They wound their way into the hills. The uphill climb was murderous. The trunk cut into Ruff's back. His breath was hot and labored. Jan Clark fell twice from sheer exhaustion. Downhills weren't much better, and they made poor time, infuriating Charlie MacDonald.

"Move it. I won't lose my scalp to some Cheyenne renegade."

"You could hide the gold," Jan suggested hopefully.

"I'm not leaving it. Damned if I'll do that."

"Charlie," Kent said in a whisper, "there's someone back there. I heard a horse."

"You sure?" Charlie's eyes flashed and he half-spun around. "Sure you don't have the heebie-jeebies again?"

"If I do, the heebie-jeebies are riding horseback."

Charlie made a sound through his teeth and turned back to Justice as if all of this were his fault. "Move out, tall man. Damn you, you keep moving."

"The girl can't do much more. One of you will have to carry her trunk for a time," Justice said.

It was true. Jan stood beside her trunk, weaving on her feet. Charlie looked at Kent and the younger outlaw backed away a step.

"Now, Charlie . . ."

"Now Charlie, hell! Shoulder that. If the girl can do it, you can. Just think of all the whiskey and all the women that gold'll buy us in Denver."

At that moment Kent didn't care much about

130

Denver, whiskey, or women, but he shouldered the trunk and shifted it, his face a mask.

"Scout, I said get going," Charlie repeated, and Ruff started on, trudging down the trail, a silent Tata on his right as they wound through the massive, rain-thick pines.

"I think we lost 'em," Charlie said hopefully after a while. "Stone Eyes don't know where we are. Why would he care anyway?" The outlaw spoke as if it were an incantation. Perhaps Charlie MacDonald was trying to keep his own heebie-jeebies at bay.

It rained, briefly, a squall that swept in through the pines, soaked them to the bones, and moved on again, chuckling away through the trees.

Three hours later they saw the light and held up at the top of a wooded hill, panting.

"That's the Triple C," MacDonald said.

"Indians haven't hit it. If they had, we'd see fire," Kent pointed out. He was rubbing his shoulder. Justice knew how he felt. His own back was dripping blood now. Tata, crouched down, arms folded on his knees, seemed impervious to pain and exhaustion. As Ruff watched, he fingered the leg of his hide trousers once, touching the twisted arrow he had hidden there.

"Let's get on down," Charlie said. "What're we waiting for?"

"Give us a break, Charlie," Kent said. "That's another mile on."

"Let's move," Charlie said, and again the authority in his voice cowed his brother. They started on down through the pines, Jan still moving unsteadily despite the fact that Kent was carrying her load.

Kent himself was unnerved. He continued to say that he heard horses behind them. Justice could hear nothing above the wind, so he figured it was imagination. Maybe.

Triple C was a fair-sized ranch, its main house damaged by fire, one corral knocked down, and the barn burned out. The light they had seen came from the front room of the house. As they straggled out of the trees, the front door opened and Charlie held them up with a hand signal.

Kent lowered his trunk, rubbed his shoulder again, and checked out his rifle.

"Cribbs," Charlie said softly.

A big-shouldered man with a considerable limp had come out of the house. As they watched, he rounded the corner and returned with a string of horses. Three of them were saddled. Inside the house Justice saw a woman moving around hurriedly, as if she were making preparations to leave.

"Just the ticket," Charlie MacDonald said. "Kent, hold 'em here."

"What're you going to do?"

"Talk to the man."

As they watched, Charlie MacDonald walked across the ranch yard toward the house. Hearing footsteps, Cribbs looked around sharply.

They could hear the voices of the two men clearly in the pines as they waited under Kent MacDonald's gun.

"Scared hell out of me, mister. There's Cheyenne around, you know. Got the word from Ben Pyle out of Clear Creek. They burned his place again."

Charlie MacDonald answered casually, "That's not news to me. Ran me off my digs tonight. Got my cousin."

"Prospecting, are you?" Cribbs asked. The bay he was holding backed away a little, and the rancher briefly turned his attention to it.

"That's right."

"Others have tried it around here, doesn't get them much. See any color?"

"A little," Charlie answered softly.

"Where you at?" Cribbs wanted to know. "Didn't know anyone was panning around here."

"Down at Twin Buttes."

"That so?" Cribbs sounded suddenly uneasy. "Well, I'm glad you made it out. Sorry about your cousin. You'd best get yourself back to Clear Creek. That's what I'm fixing to do."

"I need horses," MacDonald said, and his Winchester had slowly shifted toward Cribbs without the rancher's having been aware of it.

"Everyone does. These are all I've got left."

"Six of 'em?" Charlie MacDonald said, looking toward the house.

"That's right. Six. Look, mister, if you want to ride to Clear Creek with us, there's a saddle in the shed around the corner there."

"That won't do," Charlie said.

"What do you mean?"

"I need more than one horse."

"Oh?" Cribbs now looked toward the pine trees suspiciously. "Well, I got six. How many do you need?"

"All of them," Charlie said. The Winchester had come up slowly, the muzzle just below the rancher's belt buckle.

Cribbs let his eyes drop. The bay moved nervously and Cribbs stroked its neck. "All of them?" he said with a nervous laugh. "I can't do that, friend. I got to get my wife and daughter to Clear Creek."

"They can walk." There was no doubt at all as to Charlie's intentions now. The Winchester was pointed at the rancher's chest, the hammer back. "Why don't you just saddle two more of these horses for me now and we'll part friends."

"Why, I'll be damned if I will, you horse thief . . ."

Cribbs took a step toward Charlie MacDonald, and Charlie shot him through the heart. The rancher was blown back against his porch and he lay still, arms outstretched.

Inside the house someone screamed and the front door opened. Kent MacDonald fired three times into the doorway and windows of the house and the door slammed shut.

"Now," Kent said to Justice, "we got us some transportation."

14

They rode on and the rain came down. The land was dark, the sky starless. Charlie MacDonald led the way, his brother bringing up the rear. One of the horses carried the gold; a dismal Jan Clark rode beside Ruff Justice. Tata might never have been on a horse before. If he had been, it didn't show.

"Where are they taking us?" Jan asked.

"North. Outside of that I've no idea. Not to Clear Creek, I wouldn't think."

"They don't need us anymore, do they, Ruff?" Jan asked.

He told her the truth. "No, Jan, they don't need us anymore."

The woman was frightened into silence. She knew now that Charlie MacDonald would kill when he took a notion. The event at the Cribbs ranch had proved that. He had no use at all for Ruff and Tata now, and the only use he and his brother could have for Jan frightened her even more when she thought of it.

Kent shouted ahead to his brother. "The stone cabin?"

"That's right."

Apparently the MacDonalds knew a hideout. Justice had no idea where they meant. He didn't figure his chances were better than fifty-fifty that he ever would know.

They rode down a narrow tree-lined valley where water sheeted over a stone bench, making a short-lived waterfall. An owl hooted at them—a strange sound, as if it were puzzled by the storm. Ruff could just make out the distant glow that must have been Clear Creek. He wondered about the town, wondered if Stone Eyes had finished his work there this time.

The war whoop sounded from up the canyon and Kent MacDonald spun in the saddle, all of his fears suddenly taking form. He fired up into the trees before he could have possibly had a target.

In another minute he had all the targets he could use. The renegades flowed out of the trees and down the mountainside like a living tide. Kent continued to fire, his bullets grooving the stormy night with flame.

His brother was shouting wildly, "Dammit, Kent! Ride, ride. We haven't got a chance in hell out here."

Ruff grabbed the bridle to Jan's horse, the same nervous bay that had given Cribbs trouble, lined it out, and lifted his own horse into a dead-out run. He hoped those Indians were riding tired ponies.

Charlie MacDonald seemed to know where he was going. They followed him down an even narrower feeder canyon, up onto a grassy bench and then to the stone house, which stood solidly unconcerned before the deep ranks of pines rising behind it.

Ruff swung down on the run, reaching for Jan. Charlie MacDonald was already down, firing over his head toward the Cheyenne raiders.

"Forget the woman, grab the gold," Charlie said. He had lost his hat and the wind stood his sandy hair up on his head. He looked like some dark, slickered rain demon, his face twisted with tension.

Ruff grabbed the gold trunk from its hasty sling on

the back of the pack horse, grabbed Jan's as well, and ran, dragging his load behind him toward the cabin door. Tata was on his heels. The two outlaws covered them with fire from their repeating rifles, backing toward the cabin.

Kent was tagged. He was hunched over, firing blindly. He had taken lead in the belly, and when he reached the door, he practically fell inside, cursing and shouting angrily.

Charlie MacDonald kicked the door shut, dropped the bar, and went to one of the narrow slit windows, emptying his rifle into the dark mass of milling renegades outside. The Cheyenne had turned and run before Charlie had gotten his Colt up. Gone and taken their horses with them.

"God damn it all, God damn it all," Kent Mac-Donald kept shouting.

"Shut up!" his brother yelled.

"Shut up! Shut up? I've got lead in my guts, Charlie."

"And if you don't shut up, I'll finish it." Charlie MacDonald was shoveling cartridges into his rifle, dropping three of them in his haste.

"They gone?" Kent asked.

"For now. They took the horses."

"They won't be back," Kent said hopefully. "They know they can't get us out of here."

As if to belie that statement a barrage of Indian gun-fire shocked the night, ricochets whining off the stone walls, bullets thudding into the heavy oaken door.

Charlie MacDonald ducked away from the narrow window, turning his back to the wall. But he had seen gunfights before and he wasn't intimidated. He twisted around again, poked the muzzle of his repeater out the window, and fired three times.

Crouching, he moved to the window on the other

side of the door, cutting loose a few rounds from there. "At least they'll think we got two warriors," Charlie grunted.

"Let me have a gun," Ruff Justice said.

Charlie looked at him as if he were mad. "You go to hell, Justice! Sit in that corner with the woman and the monkey and stay there."

Jan Clark asked, "What about your brother?"

Charlie looked uncertainly at Kent, who had flopped on the cot in the corner, blood leaking through his fingers.

"All right." Charlie went to where his brother lay, removed his weapons, and said, "See what you can do, lady."

The outlaw returned to the window, his brother's rifle propped up beside him, the extra pistol shoved into his belt. He shed his rain slicker finally, revealing a white shirt with the elbows out. Jan was opening Kent MacDonald's shirt. The man lay groaning, writhing.

"Justice?" Jan whispered when she had gotten the shirt open.

Charlie MacDonald turned his eyes to Ruff, who was still in the corner. The outlaw nodded almost imperceptibly and Ruff went to the cot to examine the wound.

"I've never . . ." Jan was ready to faint, and Justice didn't blame her. It was low in the guts and nasty. The bullet must have hit something, maybe Kent's rifle, before entering. A jagged, searing hot piece of lead had torn his belly like a can opener.

Kent lifted his head and looked hopefully at Ruff Justice. There was sweat standing out in pearls on his forehead. "Well?" he demanded in a choked voice.

"We'll bandage it up," Justice said.

138

"What do you mean, bandage it up? Is that all you can do?"

"That's all anyone could do," Justice said.

"Damn it all. Damn it all to flaming hell!"

"I told you to shut up," Charlie said from across the darkened cabin. "Now, shut up!"

Charlie was beginning to crack a little too. He had his gold, but he had lost his cousin and was about to lose his brother. Outside, he had a renegade army, and it wasn't just going to go away and leave him alone to make his way to Denver and his women and whiskey.

"Tie him up tight," Charlie said to Justice. "Then, Kent, you get yourself over to this window."

"I can't stand."

"You'll stand, damn you, and you'll fight. Do it, Justice."

"Give me a gun," Ruff repeated, and for a moment Charlie MacDonald seemed to consider the suggestion. But he shook his head and turned his eyes toward the darkness outside the slit window. "You won't make it this way," Justice said. "They'll break the door down."

"Shut up!"

"I can shut up, but it won't solve anything," Ruff Justice answered. "Your brother can't fight. I can."

"And turn the gun on me."

"That would leave me in the same situation," Ruff said.

"Forget it—shut up and forget it." Charlie MacDonald found a target outside somewhere and let a single bullet fly. There was no telling if he hit anything or not. There was no answer from outside guns. The renegades had settled in to wait out the whites.

Kent made a liar out of Justice. Somehow the outlaw had gotten to his feet, and with his guts leaking from his body—despite the futile bandage Jan had made from the hem of her skirt—he staggered to the window, caught the rifle his brother tossed him, and settled in to fight. He was green and trembling, but perhaps Kent figured if he fought he had some chance. Some chance of getting out of there and to a doctor. He had none at all if the Cheyenne got to the cabin.

"Now," Charlie MacDonald told Ruff triumphantly, "sit down like I told you."

Justice sat on the floor, his arms looped around his legs. Jan was beside him, pale and tousled. Tata sat staring, thinking his own thoughts.

The Cheyenne came in again. The bullets rang off the stone walls and Charlie MacDonald answered their fire. One stray ricochet found its way through the slit window and sang a brief, deadly tune before falling, spent, on the floor.

"This side," Kent shouted, but there was nothing his brother could do to help him out with the angle the windows gave. Kent emptied his rifle frantically. He was a killer, but he was no soldier.

The Indian's face appeared in the window and Charlie MacDonald fired into it, blowing away flesh and bone. Ruff heard the sound on the roof and he looked up.

"Up there," he called to Charlie, who spun and sent three rounds through the plank and sod roof of the cabin. A thump followed that and the raider rolled off and onto the ground.

"Give me a gun!" Justice pleaded again, and again Charlie MacDonald shook his head. He kept firing from the window until a second lull, sudden and as unnerving as the rifle fire, settled.

Charlie pulled away from the window, his face darkened by powder smoke. "Pushed 'em back," he said with satisfaction.

"How far?" Ruff asked. "They can wait, can't they? They've got food and water. We haven't."

"What do you want me to do, Justice? Burrow my way out? I'll stand 'em till someone shows up."

"Who? The law?"

"Maybe. And maybe they'll find a dead man, a dead woman, and a monkey. Who's to say the renegades didn't get 'em? Now you sit there"—a stubby finger pointed at Ruff—"sit there and keep your mouth shut."

Kent nearly fell from his position at the window as he tried to reload his gun. There was no way the kid was going to last long. Charlie looked at him as if Kent were somehow responsible for getting himself shot and ruining his plans.

"What good is the gold going to do you?" Jan Clark asked suddenly. "What good is any of this?"

"We'll see. Maybe plenty of good. Maybe good enough to set me up for life. One good haul, lady. That's all a man needs. This is my chance for it, and I'm damned if anyone's going to take it away from me. Stone Eyes, you, or that damned buckskinned scout."

"I wouldn't touch it," Jan answered, and she looked at the trunks in the corner as if they were rotten meat.

"You say that now, lady," Charlie said, "but you tell me—just what was it you wanted at the buttes if it wasn't that gold?"

"You wouldn't understand," Jan replied.

"No, I don't understand," Charlie said with heavy sarcasm. "You can fool the scout, maybe, but you can't fool me, lady. It's gold. Everyone wants gold."

"Charlie," Kent said with absolute weariness, "they're coming again."

The night plodded past: interludes of silence and darkness punctuated by sudden sound and fire. Ruff had to hand it to the MacDonalds: they were doing some fighting. And when the fighting was over and they had time to think about the fate of their prisoners . . . ?

Justice couldn't wait that long.

Kent was dying on his feet, but he still had a gun and was still dangerous. Charlie was exhausted from his bloody vigil, but he was alert enough that Justice didn't want to try slipping up on him.

"Something's got to be done," Jan whispered to Ruff.

"What?"

"There has to be a way."

No, there didn't have to be. There wasn't always a way to do these things without getting someone killed, but Jan was right: they had to try it. Otherwise it was obvious what was going to happen to them. Maybe with Stone Eyes they had a chance.

Maybe.

"Here they come afoot," Kent MacDonald called out, and his brother turned wearily to the window. The rifles from outside summoned answering fire. The sky seemed to catch the sparks of the guns and take color. Justice realized it was nearly dawn. Time.

He slowly drew his feet under him. Now, while the Cheyenne had the MacDonalds' attention. Jan's hand reached out and gripped Ruff's sleeve, but he shook her off. He had his eyes on Kent MacDonald. If he could get to Kent and take his gun, he had a chance against Charlie MacDonald. Kent wasn't capable of putting up much of a fight himself.

Ruff rose to a crouch now, his eyes on Charlie. He was spacing his rounds, picking off the Cheyenne when he saw them, not firing blindly into the night. Charlie MacDonald was a cool customer, a fighting man. It wasn't going to be easy.

Ruff took one quick running step and Charlie

142

whirled, his eyes narrowing to slits. He turned his gun on Justice but never got the chance to use it.

Tata was a blur of motion as he hurled himself at Charlie MacDonald. The twisted arrow flashed through the air, driven downward by Tata's fist, and was buried in Charlie's throat. The outlaw staggered back and fell against the wall, his white shirt flooded with crimson blood.

"Charlie!" Kent MacDonald spun and his rifle spoke loudly in the confines of the cabin. A bullet ripped through the body of the cave dweller, slamming him backward in a jumbled somersault.

Kent tried to shift his rifle, but he was too late. Justice was already on top of him. Ruff slammed his forearm into the outlaw's face and ripped the rifle free with his left hand. Kent tried to fight back, reaching for his handgun. Justice triggered off and the Winchester boomed, sending spinning death through Kent MacDonald's battered body.

Rifle fire peppered the walls of the cabin again and Justice got to a window. He saw an onrushing Cheyenne, his figure black and unreal against the dawn-streaked sky. Justice settled the front sight of the rifle on the dark figure and squeezed off. The renegade Cheyenne crumpled up and lay still.

Jan had crawled across the cabin floor to Tata's body. She turned and looked at Justice, her face anguished.

"Dead," she said hoarsely. "Dead."

But there was a smile on Tata's face. He had died a warrior, helping his friends. Maybe the only friends he had ever had. The Cheyenne made a desultory charge and Ruff beat them back one more time with rapid fire. Then they were gone, leaving the dead outside. Justice turned to the dead within the cabin and to the woman who, trembling violently, threw herself into his arms and sobbed for a long time.

Dawn was crimson and gold against the towering clouds that still drifted southward across the pine hills. Wearing two gun belts now and holding a rifle, Justice stared out at the open grassland before them.

"Gone?" Jan asked hopefully.

"I can't tell for sure. Seems like it. If we had horses, I'd almost be tempted to try getting out of here."

"We could walk out." She looked at the bodies strewn around the cabin floor. "I can't stay in here much longer. I'm afraid I'll go to pieces."

"I'll take them outside," Ruff said. He handed her the rifle.

"Is it safe?"

"Not very," Justice admitted. Nor was it very comfortable sharing the cabin with the dead. Charlie MacDonald's open eyes seemed to watch them wherever they moved, as if he would suddenly leap up and go for their throats. But it was Tata's body that bothered them both. Tata, the last of a race, brought out into the bloody modern world to die uselessly.

Ruff opened the door tentatively. There was no sound but jays squawking in the pines. The wind ruffled the long grass in front of the cabin gently. He took a deep breath. "I'll give it a try," he said.

He hooked Charlie MacDonald under the arms and dragged the body to the door.

Bert Skye stood there, shotgun in his hands. Beside him was Doc Plimpton, carrying a Colt.

"Thanks. I was wondering how to break that door down," Skye said. "Drop the rifle, lady."

Ruff backed away as Skye entered, the muzzle of the scattergun moving around like a hound sniffing at the corners of the room. Jan had dropped her gun and stepped away from it.

Skye still wore his diamond ring and stickpin, but his black suit was stained, his hat torn. The saloon-keeper couldn't help noticing the dead men—noticing and approving.

"Thanks again, Justice. I was wondering how we were going to convince Charlie to turn that gold over to us." He looked at Doc Plimpton and winked. Plimpton, a revolver in either hand, didn't respond. He was like one of the dead himself, or like an undertaker. The gunman eased into the cabin, his pale eyes switching from point to point erratically before lighting again on Justice. "Take those pistols off, Justice."

"Where's August Delight?" Ruff asked, unbuckling his gun belt.

"The big man couldn't keep up," Skye answered.

Ruff eyed Skye steadily. "What do you mean?"

"He couldn't keep up." Skye barked a laugh. "Being dead."

"You killed him?"

Skye nodded toward Doc Plimpton. The pale-eyed gunman's mouth twitched.

"Why?" Justice asked. His mouth was dry, his hands clenching.

"He didn't move quick enough. It doesn't matter why now—he said something to Doc, and that was that. It usually is with Doc."

Again the gunman's mouth twitched and Justice had to fight to hold himself back. He wanted nothing more in the world just then than to smash his fist into the mad gunfighter's face. August Delight had been a big, good-natured, hardworking man with a wife and four kids. This slimy thing had killed him, apparently over a trivial incident.

"You'll pay," Justice said under his breath. "If I ever get the chance to draw on you, you'll pay, Plimpton."

Plimpton didn't hear him, nor did Skye, who had

145

toed open one of the gold trunks. Ruff heard his breath catch. "See, Doc," he said. "I told you so, didn't I? Knew the lady would find that gold. Knew what the MacDonalds were up to. I told you—we're rich, Doc, rich."

Plimpton didn't seem to care. He only seemed to want to kill somebody, anybody. Ruff Justice seemed the likely candidate.

15

....•———◆———•....

"What are you going to do with us?" Jan Clark asked. The fear seemed to have gone out of her. Maybe you can be afraid only so long before it turns to anger. Her color was up as she asked Bert Skye the direct question.

"Nothing, lady. Nothing at all."

"Then, what?"

"We still need a camp hand. Justice'll do for now. Doc and I have a very long trip planned, a trip west."

"How far west?"

"San Francisco." Skye finally quit staring at the gold in the chests. When he turned toward Ruff and Jan, his eyes still seemed to hold a golden glow.

"I am not going to San Francisco," Jan exploded.

"Yes you are, lady. We're taking you because Doc here has some aversion to killing women. We can't simply let you go because of that. You'll be all right if you mind your own business. So will Justice—I guess he understands now what happens to anyone who crosses Doc."

Jan wanted to argue a little more, but Justice touched her arm and shook his head. "Anything's better than being left here dead, Jan," he told her.

She looked at him with disappointment, and Skye

laughed. "You see, Justice knows what's good for him. He won't be any trouble, will he, Doc?"

The gunman's answer was laconic. "He was trouble enough to the MacDonalds."

"That's true," Skye said thoughtfully. "Very true. We just won't let ourselves get careless. For now, I suggest we hastily vamoose before those renegades come back. When Doc and I saw them last they were heading for Clear Creek, but there might be more of them around somewhere."

"Let's go," Doc said to Justice. He still held two Colts in his pale, narrow hands.

"Where?"

"Horses are in the trees. Start carrying the gold out," Plimpton said; for him that was a dissertation.

Justice hefted the heaviest of the three trunks, feeling it bite into the old cuts. Then, under the guns of Doc Plimpton, he started out the door, Doc moving carefully away from him. He hadn't forgotten the MacDonalds.

"Feel like a slave," Justice said. "Like the Mac-Donalds sold me to you." Doc Plimpton didn't answer. He wasn't the friendliest of men. Nor was he in any sort of condition. He was puffing by the time they reached the horses in the pines behind the house. One of the horses was August Delight's.

"Rig somethin' up," Doc said.

Ruff rigged something up: a pair of slings made of harness leather for one of the horses. It wasn't made up real well, but Doc didn't seem to notice. He was no outdoorsman, no craftsman. He'd spent his life in saloons and back alleys; so had Skye. It was no wonder they needed Delight or Justice along.

"You ever seen the Rockies, Doc?" Justice asked as he strapped on the treasure chest. His fingers slid to the buckles.

148

"No."

"You will. That's a hell of a trip Skye has in mind, you know."

"Skye's the boss," was all Doc said. Then he waved his gun and they started back for a second trunk. On the last trip Jan came along, Bert Skye holding her arm. He was saying something she didn't like at all; she tried to pull away but Skye yanked her back.

Justice started that way, but the ratcheting of Doc's Colt stopped him. "Leave well enough alone, Justice, hear me?"

It galled Justice, but he had no choice. He stood his ground. After a minute Skye let go of Jan, laughing as she folded her arms and stamped on.

"You ever meet Clive Hickam, Doc?" Ruff Justice asked.

"Who? Oh, that one. I seen him."

"Didn't kill him, did you?"

Doc smiled very slowly. "With an arrow?"

"No, I guess not." Justice still hadn't figured out who killed Clive and now it looked like he wouldn't.

Skye put Jan up on a horse and let his hand linger on her thigh. Jan Clark stared away at the distances, and Skye, shrugging, went to his own horse.

"Take that one, Justice, the sorrel. It don't run good."

Justice swung aboard obediently. Skye looked at Ruff. "Which way, scout?"

"Skye, do you know what kind of trip you're talking about? A thousand miles in rough country without sufficient supplies. Over the mountains, where you've got every chance of hitting early snow."

"I guess I know. You'll get us through—you'd better. Matter of fact, Justice, I'll tell you what: you get us through and I'll give you ten thousand dollars. How about that?" His eyes shifted to Jan. "And the woman."

Ruff appeared to think it over. He didn't trust Skye but that was all right. Skye wasn't going to half-trust him. "A man could live long on ten thousand, long and well."

"That's right. You remember that, scout. Remember one other thing as well." He nodded to the gunfighter. "Doc never misses. Ever."

"I'll remember. I don't suppose that leaves a smart man much of a choice. Get rich or get dead." Justice smiled.

"That's about it."

"Let's ride, then. Better let me take the lead."

"Which way are you taking us?" Skye wanted to know.

"Over Dalton Ridge."

"South?"

"The farther we are from the Cheyenne, the better I'll feel," Justice answered.

Skye was uncertain. "That's pretty rough country, isn't it?"

"It's all rough," Justice answered. "It'll take us south and near to Frenchman's Pass. Once we get that far, you won't have to worry about anyone picking up your back trail—Cheyenne or white."

"I'm not worried about the law now, or the army. No one knows about this gold or Delight except you and the lady. There won't be anyone following us."

"Don't be so sure," Ruff Justice said. "That's just what Charlie MacDonald thought, and you found him. Where there's this much gold there'll be someone looking."

Ruff Justice was talking through his hat. No one could possibly know about the gold, no one who could track them down, but it wouldn't hurt to work on

Skye's nerves a little, let him worry. Ruff Justice was in the lead now, Skye with a shotgun behind him. It was a good thing Skye was such a town rat. He had echoed something he must have heard once: that Dalton Ridge was a rough piece of ground. It wasn't that—it was savage and raw, and the trail Justice meant to take was one of the most hazardous in the Badlands.

The trail they rode now slanted up and away from the timbered valley where the stone cabin lay. To the south Justice could see Twin Buttes. From time to time, looking over his shoulder, he could make out Clear Creek, a town that seemed doomed. It had survived Stone Eyes' first attack by the skin of its teeth.

It would take a miracle to keep Clear Creek alive this time.

Ahead, the Badlands began to form. The green timber gave way to gray twisted trees and red earth, to deeply cut, winding arroyos and waterless plateaus. Dalton Ridge rose challengingly across their path; serrated, massive and purple in the early light.

Ruff twisted in his saddle and saw Skye staring back, shotgun in hand, uneasy expression on his face. Jan Clark was behind him, then Doc Plimpton and the pack horses.

The trail rose sharply along the face of a red bluff. Below, a green river wound its way toward the Heart—a nameless, characterless river that existed only on maps and after a heavy rainfall. An hour later, the river was five hundred feet below them. A rock on the edge of the trail crumbled away and fell down the long red slopes beneath the horses' hooves.

Skye was in a sweat. "Dammit, Justice, if this is some kind of stinking trick, I'll kill you."

"What kind of a trick?" Ruff asked blandly. "You

think I want to die? The trail's a little narrow here. It'll get better."

It didn't. As Justice knew it would, the trail took a sharp upward bend and narrowed still more. There was hardly room for a horse to walk. Nothing green was in sight above them, only an occasional dead tree, twisted junipers, and stunted pines.

"Maybe we'd better walk," Justice said.

Skye's face was white with fear. He tried to bluster but he didn't have it in him. Below, the earth fell away six hundred feet or more to the narrow ribbon of green river. Above, the bluff rose steeply, cutting out the sun.

"We should go back, is what we should do," Skye said.

"Fine. Let me see you turn your horse."

"What's happening up there?" Doc Plimpton demanded.

"We're going to walk," Skye shouted.

"Walk—dammit!" Plimpton wasn't a walking man. Not the sort to walk this grade, leading three horses.

Ruff got down over the haunches of the sorrel. There wasn't room enough to swing over. Easing past, he led his horse upward. The sorrel wasn't used to mountain trails either, and he didn't like it a bit.

Neither did Skye. "How far now?" he panted. "How far to where it widens out?"

"Not far," Justice said cheerfully.

Skye looked as if he'd have liked to shoot him then and there. The saloon keeper was leading his horse along the trail. Glancing back, Ruff saw what he had been waiting for. Doc Plimpton, laboring to climb the trail, had fallen well behind. A bend in the trail cut the gunfighter's line of vision.

Ruff halted, took the sorrel by the bridle, and

started backing the horse. Skye looked up, his eyes growing wide and frightened.

"What are you doing, what's happening?"

Justice kept moving the horse back. Now its rump moved between the wall of the bluff and Skye. Skye's own horse reared up and flailed at the air with its front hooves.

"Justice!" Skye called, but Ruff showed the man no mercy. The backing sorrel gave Skye another nudge and he went over, cartwheeling through space, a long moaning scream escaping his lips.

The lead horses panicked. Justice pressed himself against the wall of the bluff. He saw Jan go down flat on the trail, the horses picking their way over her. And Doc Plimpton was coming on the run.

He looked more like a cadaver than ever. He wasn't built for running up hillsides. The Colt in his hand never wavered as he brought it up, however. He fired, the bullet ringing off the sandstone bluff. Justice dived for the scattergun Skye had dropped, rolled to a sitting position, and cut loose with both barrels. Doc Plimpton was blown off the trail into the emptiness below.

Jan rose shakily, looking dirty but unharmed. Ruff rose and walked to Jan, who remained sitting on the earth, her feet in space.

"I thought Skye said his gunfighter never missed," she said.

"Just once."

Ruff gave her his hand and pulled her up. She clung to him for a time while the wind gusted around them. Justice still held the scattergun, empty now, but it had served its purpose.

After the long hike and the climb up the trail, Doc Plimpton's aim hadn't been what it was when he was braced in an alley or ready to shoot from beneath his

poker table. Ruff hadn't had his problem. It was difficult to miss a man at thirty feet with a shotgun. Justice
hadn't missed.

Jan pulled suddenly away from Ruff and pointed
behind them. "Ruff, the gold! It's gone."

"Is it?" Justice asked.

"The pack horses. Where are they?"

"Down the trail, but they didn't carry their packs
with them. I made those up myself. I'm surprised they
lasted this long."

"Then the trunks . . ." She peered downward, into
the chasm.

"I'll hold your feet if you want to look for them,"
Justice said.

"Why? Why did you do it?" Jan asked.

"I thought it might give us an opportunity to make
something happen if the gold fell from the horses. We
needed some kind of chance. I didn't plan on this—
that gold is scattered to hell and gone down that
slope."

"You don't even care, do you? You really don't care
that it's gone."

"No," Justice said honestly, "I don't care. Maybe
it's back where it belongs. With the lost ones."

He was looking out across the hills, and Jan shook
her head, not understanding. A shiny object on the
trail caught her eye and she stooped to recover it. A
single coin, a single piece of Spanish gold.

"The diary was in one of those trunks, Ruff. It's
gone. Tata's gone. The gold's gone."

"I guess so. Everything's gone. You can go back to
the buttes, I suppose, drag out the armor or Father
Aguilar's remains, prove that your father wasn't
wrong."

"I don't need to." The woman shook her head. The

154

wind drifted her dark hair across her pretty face. "*I* know he was right. All of a sudden that's enough."

Then she drew back her arm and sent the coin sailing off into space. It turned in the sunlight, winking brightly before falling into the shadowed chasm. "I think enough people have died for that gold," Jan Clark said.

"I think so."

That was all Justice said before he took her by the elbow and turned her back down the trail, back toward Clear Creek, leaving the secrets of the cave dwellers behind, leaving the Spanish gold scattered across the vast, barren hillside.

16

Clear Creek was burning. They could see the smoke from five miles out. Stone Eyes, angered at the temerity of the town and its people, was determined to crush both. This time there would be nothing but ashes and bone when the renegade was through with his bloody work.

"Fort Lincoln?" Jan asked. They stood beside their horses, watching the distant smoke. "Can we make it that far?"

"Not across the prairie. We wouldn't have a chance in hell."

"Where, then?" the lady asked. The lady who had changed so much, who had lost her temper and her brittle manners, who had practically become a different person out here.

Where was a good question. They couldn't hope to make Lincoln, couldn't stay in the hills, couldn't return to the caves, where presumably some of the Cheyenne were still holed up.

Ruff tried to gauge the fire, to see exactly what was burning. It seemed to be grass smoke for the most part. Probably Stone Eyes, held off temporarily by the citizens of Clear Creek, had started several grass fires to drive them out. By now, perhaps some of the buildings had caught again.

"What's that?" Jan asked, lifting a pointing finger to the east. "Is that cavalry? Help coming?" Her voice rose hopefully.

Justice had to burst her bubble. "It's not cavalry." Squinting into the sun he could just make out what it was. "Freight wagons. A dozen of them rolling toward Clear Creek."

"Shouldn't they be warned?"

"They can see the smoke as well as we can. They know what's happening. Come on."

"Where?" Jan asked, puzzled.

"If we're going to have to fight, I don't want to do it alone. Let's see what those teamsters have in mind."

Jan didn't argue. Ruff had made a decision—a right one or a wrong one, but one that had to be made. They swung aboard their horses and headed for the wagon road, where the mule teams were rolling toward Clear Creek, driven by men who had families and friends there.

They caught them this side of Red Springs. The drivers, armed and grim, weren't slowing down for anything or anybody. Ruff managed to swing aboard the lead wagon, leaving Jan to trail behind with his horse.

The teamster was Joe Carroll, his swamper Ed Hughes. Both men had a wife and children at Clear Creek.

"See anything of what's happening, Ruff?" Carroll yelled above the rumble of wheels, the thundering of hooves, the rattle of trace chains and shifting of his cargo.

"Nothing but the smoke, same as you."

"Didn't bring a horse-soldier patrol with you, did you?"

"Not this time," Ruff said. "It's up to us."

"Stone Eyes, is it?" Ed Hughes shouted.

"Must be. Joe, I think we'd better stop for a minute and have us a talk."

"No time, Ruffin." The teamster lashed his mules. They took a sharp bend in the road and started into the pines.

"There's always time for common sense, Joe. We can't just roll on into Clear Creek. Stone Eyes'll damn sure have seen your dust. He'll be waiting."

Joe Carroll was an impetuous man, used to hard work and hard fighting. He was also a man with some brains. "All right. You're right, I reckon, Justice." He began to slow his team, holding up his hand to halt the wagons behind him before he nodded to his swamper, who started applying the brakes to the big wagon's wheels.

They halted in the pines, throwing up clouds of dust and fountains of pine needles as, one behind the other, the heavy wagons skidded to a squealing stop.

"What in the hell is going on?"

A big-shouldered, square-faced man with a whip in his hand and two pistols crossed on his hips reached Carroll's wagon before the dust had settled.

"Settle, Stansford," Joe told him. "Justice here thinks we ought to have us a quick war conference. He's right."

"A conference. We go in shooting, that's all," the other man said.

"Stansford?" Ruff Justice said, climbing down. "May Stansford's husband."

"That's right. And you're Ruff Justice, so what?" the teamster asked belligerently.

Jan had made her way up to where Justice stood talking to the teamster. Other men, anxious, dust-coated, had gathered around.

"Nothing," Ruff said. "I'd just heard your name."

"I've heard yours. How's that help us fight Stone Eyes?"

Ruff's mouth tightened. No wonder May Stansford hadn't mentioned her husband. "It doesn't help. Neither does rushing in there madly. He'll know we're coming. Let's try to use some sense and get organized."

"Think there's time for that?" Stansford's arm lifted, a finger jabbed westward. "Our town's burning."

"Dying won't help stop that. Joe?" He turned to Carroll.

"It's your show, you're the Indian fighter." Carroll nodded.

"For one thing you've got too many wagons. You can't drive and shoot at the same time. Some of these rigs are going to have to be left behind."

"Leave our goods?"

"Sorry. You'll be lucky if you salvage any of them anyway," Justice told them. "You've got to have men ready and able to shoot. Take the first four wagons, everyone else in the back. Barricade yourselves with the crates as best you can and we'll roll through. If Stone Eyes doesn't take the mules down, we should make it. Drivers, work from the boxes. He'll try to pick you off first."

"I'm damned if I'll leave my goods," Stansford said. "Not on *his* say-so."

"Use your brains, Luke," Joe Carroll said, "not your mouth. Taking those goods through isn't going to help anybody if Clear Creek's burned to the ground."

"Damn you," Luke Stansford said. For a minute Ruff thought he was going to hit Carroll, but Joe Carroll wasn't a man you challenged lightly.

Ed Hughes broke it up. "For God's sake, my wife's

up ahead. Am I going to have to stand here and watch some asinine argument?"

"Let's do it," another man said. "I'm willing to leave my rig. I'd sooner shoot than drive just now. As for that lumber I'm carrying, let Stone Eyes make himself a heap big bonfire, what do I care?"

"We're doing it your way, I guess, Ruff," Joe said. "Want to ride along?"

"If you've got an extra rifle."

Joe Carroll grinned. "Break open one of those flat crates. We're carrying Winchesters."

Men began shifting crates, changing wagons. Ruff climbed into Carroll's wagon, tugging Jan up beside him.

"Do I get a rifle?" she asked.

"Can you hit anything?"

"I'm willing to try. You've got plenty of guns and ammunition, don't you? I can make a lot of noise anyway."

Ruff opened a crate of rifles, tossed away the oiled paper they were wrapped in, checked the bore, and handed a .44–40 needle gun to Jan.

"Cartridges are there. It'll take sixteen in the magazine. Anything with feathers you shoot at."

"I can figure it out," Jan said. "I've seen some shooting lately, enough to know what the lever's for."

Ruff smiled, kissed her quickly on the forehead, and began shoving cartridges into his own weapon. Joe Carroll had the brake off, the wagon rolling before everyone was on board and settled. Up ahead, smoke columned into the cloud-dappled sky.

"Keep it pointed that way," Justice shouted to Jan. "Remember, you haven't got those spectacles of yours anymore."

Jan offered him a tense smile in return. She would

be all right, he decided. The lady would be all right from here on out.

They crested the pine ridge and saw Clear Creek spread before them. Ruff's guess that the fire was mostly grass so far proved to be right. They could see the red flames winking and curling behind the screen of black smoke. So far only the stable on the west end of town seemed to be threatened, and it was there that Stone Eyes' renegades appeared, leading the all-valuable horses from the fire.

It was too far for any sort of decent shot, but Justice settled in on the bouncing bed of the wagon and put half a dozen rounds through the barrel of his Winchester, holding it three feet high. Might as well let them know there was going to be a fight.

"The hotel," Joe Carroll shouted.

It was from there that the answering fire came. Most of the town seemed to be holed up in the hotel and rifles blazed from every window.

As they rolled nearer, they could see Cheyenne raiders moving through the alleys and across rooftops. Farther out on the plains were dozens of men on horseback, waiting for their leader's signal to charge, to finish the siege-battered town once and for all.

"Get your heads down," Justice shouted to the men in his wagon. Jan Clark was too interested in seeing the sights and Ruff had to shove her head down. She complained, but not for long as the wagons hit the main street at full bore and the Cheyenne rifles opened up.

Bullets slammed into the crates protecting the teamsters from the rooftop snipers. Ruff Justice rolled onto his back and picked a painted renegade from the roof of the dry-goods store. The Indian toppled forward, turning a slow somersault as he fell to the street, his scream sounding above the roar of repeating rifles.

The wagons jolted down the rough street, the returning teamsters filling the day with red-hot lead. Justice saw a Cheyenne raise up from behind an oak trough, saw Ed Hughes send a .44 bullet into the Cheyenne's belly. Stansford took an Indian who appeared in the window of the saddlery, and the warrior crashed through the glass to die on the boardwalk.

Then Carroll was out of the bed, slamming on the wagon brakes. The teamsters vaulted from the wagons and made for the steps of the hotel.

A Cheyenne bullet took a man in the back; he was snatched up by two other teamsters and half-carried toward the now-open door of the hotel.

"Let's go," Ruff shouted to Jan, and they went over the side of the wagon bed and into the hotel, renegade bullets chewing up boardwalk and siding around them.

Then they were inside and the shots slowed and died down. Smoke was heavy in the air. Men found their families and hugged and kissed them, reassuring wives and children. In the corner an old woman kept wailing, "How could this happen again, how could it happen?"

The stunned hotel clerk, his shirt ripped, came past.

Ruff grabbed him. "How do things stand, friend?"

"Stand?" He blinked. "Oh, it's you, Justice. Thought they must've got you. He's got us this time, don't he? Stone Eyes has got us. Smell that fire?" The clerk's head lifted. "He's got us."

Dan Woods, owner of the hotel, appeared a minute later, more under control than his clerk. With him was Gil Thomas, owner of the dry-goods store—or what was left of it.

"Meeting upstairs," Woods told Justice. "Got any ideas, you bring them along."

162

Jan Clark looked a little lost but well under control—until Jenny Farnsworth made her appearance. The young, bosomy woman saw Ruff and her mouth opened wide. She rushed across the hotel parlor and threw herself into Justice's arms.

"Ruffin, everyone thought you were dead! It's been horrible. A rider from down south came in and said that Mr. Cribbs had been killed. No one's seen Susan Cribbs or her mother . . ."

Her chattering broke off sharply as the big red-headed man came into the room. Jake Troll didn't look any more friendly than usual. He stood watching, rifle in his hands, as Jenny Farnsworth disentangled herself from Justice.

"Meeting upstairs," Troll said finally. "You too, Justice."

Ruff nodded. Jenny Farnsworth still held his sleeve. Or she did until Jan Clark gently unlocked her fingers and took Justice's arm herself, leading Ruff to the staircase. From time to time gunfire sounded and the smoke from the grass fire drifted in through shattered windows.

Upstairs the war council was meeting. Ruff walked in with Jan Clark. Besides Joe Carroll and Gil Thomas, a man called Dunwoodie, the nominal mayor of Clear Creek, was present. Still scowling, Troll tramped in behind Justice. Not long afterward Luke Stansford arrived. His wife was already there.

In the corner Clear Creek's grand dame of poetry and art sat tightly bound in linen and lace, staring with something like repugnance at her husband.

"Gentlemen," Mayor Dunwoodie began, "the current crisis . . ."

"We don't need a speech, Mayor," Joe Carroll said. "We need a plan, and right now. Stone Eyes is out there and he'll be coming in. Let a fighting man talk."

"You, Carroll?" Stansford said sourly.

"Ruff Justice. It's his business. He's army and he knows Stone Eyes better'n any of us. We're in a damned tight spot. I'd rather follow a warrior than a politician."

The mayor didn't like it, but he didn't argue. He had no suggestions of his own. Justice did, but no one was going to like his suggestion.

"Pull out," the scout said. "Give Stone Eyes the town and just pull out."

"You're crazy," Stansford shouted. "Let the bastard have everything? What would we do then?"

"We won't do it, Justice. Clear Creek is all we have."

"All you have but your lives. The lives of your families," Justice said. "I believe in fighting when you have to, when it makes sense. This doesn't. He's going to take this town—he's obsessed with the idea. No matter how long it takes, no matter how many men he loses. I *do* know Stone Eyes. The town's an insult to him. It's built on what he claims are his hunting grounds. He'll burn it, he'll bury it."

"Not if we can help it," Jake Troll said.

"But you can't, Troll, don't you see? Not now. Not with the force we have. The town, against a hundred or more armed renegades. There's no hope of help arriving from Fort Lincoln. The town's dead. All you can do is keep yourselves from being buried with it."

"This isn't your town," Luke Stansford said. "It's easy for you to say let Stone Eyes have it."

"No," Justice answered, "it isn't easy. Nor is it easy to watch your friends and family get killed, to think of women and children being scalped and tortured. You want my best advice—that's it. You people can start again. You can build a new town. For now, let the renegade have what he wants."

The mayor was trembling. He wiped at his forehead with his handkerchief. Maybe he was thinking that without a town he would be mayor of nothing.

Joe Carroll said reluctantly, "I'm afraid the man's right. Hell, boys, we can saw more timber, drive more nails, sink new wells somewhere else, if not here. I can't replace my old lady."

"I say we fight," Jake Troll said, and he looked into Ruff's eyes challengingly as he said it.

"Troll's right," Luke Stansford said.

The vote was close. Stansford and Troll almost pulled it off, almost got their wish to see everyone in Clear Creek massacred, but the cooler heads prevailed. In the end, the people of Clear Creek voted to pull out—if Stone Eyes would let them.

"That," Gil Thomas pointed out, "leaves us with a problem. Someone is going to have to go out and talk to the renegade."

"Why, that's no problem at all," Luke Stansford said with a crooked smile. "There's only one man for the job—the man who talked us into the idea in the first place: Ruff Justice."

17

---◆---

"You can't do it, Ruff," Jan Clark said. She tried to clutch his arm as he tied a white scarf to the muzzle of his Winchester repeater.

"I can't? How can I not, Jan? I don't want to see these people massacred."

"But from everything I've heard about Stone Eyes, how do you know he won't just kill you and do as he pleases anyway?"

Ruff answered soberly, "I guess I don't know that. I just don't see another chance for the people of this town. Stone Eyes will kill them all otherwise. He's made the destruction of Clear Creek into a holy objective. He'll do it. I'm hoping I can talk him into doing it the easy way."

"Let him go, lady," Luke Stansford said. "They'll send his head back on a battle lance and then we'll have it our way—a man's way, not a coward's way."

"Stansford, when I do get back, you and I have some talking to do," Ruff said.

"Do we?" the big teamster said mockingly. "I can't imagine what I'd talk to a yellow army scout about."

"Use your imagination." Ruff turned to Troll, who stood smirking beside Stansford. "That goes for you as well, Troll. I'd have thought you'd have learned something by now. I guess you haven't."

Troll answered, "I guess you won't have the time to teach me now, Justice."

He was bolstered by Stansford's antagonism. Troll was like an empty vessel; filled up with liquor or someone else's courage he could almost be taken for a man. From time to time, however, someone had to empty him out.

"Don't get killed," Jenny Farnsworth said. The little dark-haired girl looked as if she were going to go on tiptoes and kiss Justice, but a sharp glance from Jan Clark—a rather possessive glance—stopped her. "And when you come back, you teach that red-bearded man there a lesson." A dainty finger jabbed at Jake Troll, then Jenny Farnsworth turned and flounced off, ringlets bouncing.

"God, Justice," Jan Clark said, "you like them like that?"

"I like 'em like you, Doc," Ruff said, and he tilted Jan Clark's chin up, kissing her on the lips. "So long. Keep that Winchester pointed in the right direction."

Jan glanced at Farnsworth and Troll and said, "I'm not so sure I know which is the right direction. Be careful, Justice, please."

"Always," Ruff said.

Stansford was looking at Justice more intently now. He couldn't figure the scout. The closer he came to going out there alone, the calmer he seemed to become. His blue eyes were steady and cool. Ruff nodded to Joe Carroll, who was tending the door, and with a grin went out into the late sunlight, rifle held high, white scarf fluttering in the breeze.

Justice couldn't have explained it to Stansford any more than he could explain it to himself. This calm that came over him when he was closest to death—a

167

step, a breath away—was something that scared him at times. It wasn't courage exactly; it was as if his nerves just turned themselves off, the brain refusing to accept what the body was about to do.

Ruff had always been this way. Back during the war someone had mistakenly given him a medal for it. Some men a hell of a lot braver than Justice had been trembling, a few trying to run. His body just hadn't gotten the message.

Now he walked calmly out into the street and stood there, looking up and down. He saw two dead bodies: one white, one Indian.

He kept moving, walking toward the smoke of the new fire. He spotted another dead Indian lying in the dust of Clear Creek's main street.

The next ones he saw were far from dead. They stood, painted, smoke-streaked, and dusty beside the stable, their eyes on the hotel, on Ruff Justice.

"Howdy," he said in English, grinning. "Seen Stone Eyes around?"

Two of the Indians leapt for him, ripping the rifle with its truce flag from his hands. An elbow to Ruff's throat sent him sprawling, gagging, to the ground. Justice saw a war hatchet raised, saw the sunlight glint on the polished steel blade, and he figured it was the last thing he would ever see.

But the third Indian stopped the brave by grabbing his wrist. They spoke in Cheyenne.

"Stop it, he was carrying a truce flag."

"I respect no white flag. No white truce. Does Stone Eyes?"

"We will ask him."

"Let go of my arm, Fox Tooth."

"We will ask him," the other Cheyenne said, apparently outranking the first.

Slowly the Indian lowered his war hatchet.

Ruff Justice sat on the ground, holding his throat. His head rang and he shook it to clear it.

In Cheyenne he asked, "May I rise from the earth?"

"This time. Next time you will remain there until your flesh rots from your bones."

Justice rose slowly. He reached for his hat, but one of the brave's feet stretched out and stamped on it.

"Just wanted to look my best," Ruff muttered in English. Then he grinned at the warriors. "Okay, let's see my old friend Stone Eyes."

"Stone Eyes will serve your innards to his dogs," one of them said.

"Likely kill the dogs," Ruff answered. No one understood him. It didn't matter. He was going to get his wish—an interview with the butcher of the plains.

The fighting had stopped. Only the fire made war sounds. It crackled and snapped as it devoured the stable, filling the air with a tower of black smoke. Ruff walked on with his painted escort.

It was a long walk toward the oak grove along the creek. The sun blinked through the trees as it lowered itself toward the mountains. To entertain his escort Ruff Justice began to whistle. They didn't seem to appreciate it much.

More Cheyenne warriors appeared, many of them smoke-streaked, a few smeared with something of a different color, the color red.

In the center of the oak grove the most feared man on the plains stood in front of a pinto pony. He was squat, dark, powerful. Painted snakes wound their way down his arms and across his solid chest.

The eyes had given him his name, and now those eyes watched Ruff Justice. Obsidian eyes, black stone glinting behind eyelids that seemed to be merely knife slashes cut into his leather-colored skin.

Stone Eyes was watching and in his hand was a

repeating rifle; from his belt fresh scalps hung. Others decorated his leggings. Ruff Justice was taken to stand before the leader of the renegades, the reservation-schooled Cheyenne who had run away to begin his holy war. He had demonstrated the magic of his arms by gathering warriors, disaffected Cheyenne and Sioux and Arapaho, to him.

Now he stood and waited, watching the tall man in buckskins. Twenty warriors gathered around, enclosing Ruff Justice in a human noose.

Stone Eyes looked him up and down carefully. He looked and then threw back his head and roared with laughter. He pointed and through his laughter shouted, "Ruff Justice, Ruff Justice! Look who has come from out of some devil hole. Are you everywhere, Ruff Justice?"

"No, but I wouldn't mind being somewhere else just now," Ruff replied.

Stone Eyes' laughter stopped abruptly. "What are you doing here, Ruff Justice, in this dying town?"

"I've got friends here, Stone Eyes. Friends and a few enemies. My friends I want to survive to laugh with. My enemies I want to live so that I can be the one to deal with them."

"No one can survive," the renegade leader said.

"Have you taken that oath?" Ruff asked.

Stone Eyes waved a hand. Ruff noticed that three fingers were missing, a sign of grief. Those fingers had been severed by Stone Eyes himself when a loved one died. "I have taken an oath that Clear Creek shall die. It offends the spirits. If offends me. It stands where once our summer hunting camp stood. Everyone must die."

"The people are not the town," Ruff persisted. "When a man leaves a camp, he is no longer a part of it. The camp is itself. Clear Creek is those buildings, nothing more."

"You are asking me to let these people live? These white criminals?"

"I'm asking you to let a few of your warriors live. You know these people are going to fight. There are fifty of them and they all have repeating rifles. They have all the ammunition they can burn. I know because I just brought it in in a wagon."

"*You* in the wagons!" Stone Eyes laughed again. "Now I see. That was a very good move, Ruff Justice. Yes. Otherwise we should have had all the wagons, all the goods."

"You can have all the goods," Justice said. Stone Eyes weighed the idea, glancing at one of his lieutenants. "You can destroy the town and keep all the goods."

"But not the rifles."

Ruff hesitated. "Yes, the rifles. A lot of people won't like that, but I'll make that bargain with you. For the lives of the people who live here. Give us the wagons. We'll empty the goods from them and drive off. You can have the rifles, have the town."

"And if I don't agree to this"—Stone Eyes shrugged—"what does it cost me? I will have it all anyway."

"Yes, but it *will* cost you, Stone Eyes. It will cost you many warriors." Ruff pointed. "Maybe this man's life, or this one's, or that one's. Maybe all of them. Which way is the greater victory? Which way proves Stone Eyes' war magic better? To take the town, to capture those rifles without losing another warrior, or to litter the earth with your dead?"

Stone Eyes considered this. "You give me your word you will leave the rifles?"

"Yes. If you give me your word you will let us take the wagons and go."

It was a long time before Stone Eyes answered. The universe seemed to pause. "All right," he said at last. "Go, Ruff Justice. Leave the town to be burned and buried, leave it as an offering, leave the rifles and go."

Justice didn't stop to chat or ask about the family. He spun on his heel and left the grove. Stone Eyes laughed once more and Ruff wondered what in hell was so funny. Then a silent signal was passed, and Justice saw the Cheyenne renegades begin to pull back from the town.

The town of Clear Creek didn't exactly welcome Ruff Justice as a hero. Stansford was furious. "I'll not leave my damn goods, Justice."

"The hell you won't. Empty those wagons now. Get the women and kids up in the first one, turn it, and move it. Joe?"

Joe Carroll wasn't much happier. It wasn't easy for anyone to be thrilled about losing his home and all his worldly possessions.

"You can't be serious about leaving those rifles, Justice," Carroll said.

"I'm serious. It was a part of the bargain. First," Ruff added, "why don't we get us a hammer and start knocking them apart a little? Break the hammers off or the triggers."

"I thought . . ."

"Thought I'd let him use those Winchesters on someone else? Not likely. I said I'd leave the guns, gave him my word. I didn't say what kind of shape they'd be in. Let's move it now."

"Justice," Stansford said, "I'm going to kill you for this. Kill you for ruining me."

"Yeah. Some other time, Stansford. Move your butt."

As Stansford stamped away Jan Clark said, "He's serious, Ruff. He means it."

"I know he is, lady. I know it."

In fifteen minutes the streets of Clear Creek were littered with the goods the teamsters had hauled in from Bismarck. The wagons were loaded with more valuable cargo—women and kids and old people.

Joe Carroll looked down from his rig. "What's Stone Eyes going to do when he finds out you busted up those rifles, Justice?"

"Let's not wait around to find out. Move it, Joe!"

Ruff leapt into the last wagon, where Jan Clark was riding, and the freighters turned toward Bismarck, lashing their mules for all they were worth. At the crest they recovered the wagons they had left behind and rolled on. Behind them Clear Creek was still burning.

For a long while they watched the back trail as they rumbled out onto the plains, half-expecting the renegades to pursue them, but none came.

"I wonder what he thought when he found those broken rifles, Justice. He must have been furious."

"Maybe," Justice answered.

But maybe Stone Eyes had looked at the remains of his bad bargain, thrown back that ugly head of his, and laughed, loud and long—and then made a silent vow to kill Ruff Justice if ever their paths should cross again.

They rolled silently across the plains, the dust spuming up behind them. There wasn't a lot of joy among the people of Clear Creek. Twice they had been driven from their town and this time, it was unlikely that they would return.

Justice sat next to Jan Clark in the bed of the freight wagon, his arm around her. She had her knees drawn up, her arms around them. For a moment, as the

173

wagon rounded a long slow bend, they could look back and see Twin Buttes standing dark and distant and silent. They only glanced at each other, remembering Tata. Then Jan rested her head on Ruff's shoulder, leaving it there until night fell.

18

····•━━◀◆▶━━•····

Justice reported to the colonel first, advising him that Stone Eyes was moving south again, not north.

MacEnroe didn't take the time to question Justice further about events. He was rising from his desk, reaching for his saber and hat before Ruff had finished reporting.

"Going out yourself, sir?" Ruff Justice asked.

"Damn right I am. This time I'll have that bastard."

"As soon as I get a horse . . ."

"You don't look as if you could stay in the saddle, Justice," the colonel snapped. He couldn't get his saber clipped on properly and his face turned red with momentary irritation. "You stay here—that's an order." Then the colonel went out of his office shouting. "Sergeant Pierce, where is that damned bugler! I want 'boots and saddles.' I've got him, by God, and when I have him, he'll hang. Get Lieutenant Sly, by all that's holy . . ."

And then the colonel was out the orderly-room door and the office was silent. Justice sat there a long while until a yawn gapped his mouth and he shook himself. It was time to clean up. Then he was going to ride into Bismarck.

It was time to finish things up with the killer of Clive Hickam.

Justice entered the empty barracks and crossed to his trunk. Taking out soap and razor, towel and strop, bay rum and scissors, he went to the row of washbasins and began to clean up.

He wore his dark town suit and a ruffled shirt. His black hat reminded him of the stetson the renegade had stomped into the ground, and he grinned as he put it on. He was getting short on clothes; it was time to stop by the dry-goods store in Bismarck again.

He looked at the little .41 Colt New Line that rested in his trunk in its shoulder holster, and pursed his lips. It was a part of his normal evening wear, but this night might prove to be a little different than most. Ruff reached beneath a blue army blanket and removed the big gun.

He didn't wear it much, but the silver-mounted Colt Colonel Cody had given him seemed more the ticket for this evening. The .44 had a ten-inch barrel and it would take down whatever he hit. Despite the length of the barrel it came up easily from the holster, which was oiled, tooled, and hinged in the back so that the gun simply swung up and out.

Ruff whistled as he reached for his box of cartridges, but halted almost immediately. It wasn't a night for whistling, for singing, or dancing.

It was very likely a night for dying.

He looked into the steel mirror hung near the door and saw the tall figure of a man with long hair brushed neatly down across his shoulders and a carefully trimmed mustache drooping nearly to the jawline, wearing a black suit and white shirt, black string tie, and black stetson hat. The .44 looked like a gambler's rig or a circus sharpshooter's, which was the reason

Justice didn't wear it much, but it would do the job. It would definitely do the job.

Ruff took an army bay horse and rode toward Bismarck, which was well lit on this night. He knew where to find the killer of Clive Hickam—the citizens of Clear Creek had again taken refuge in the Bismarck town hall. This time, however, there was no dancing, no brass band—just a group of weary, lost people.

Ruff hitched his bay at the rail and started up onto the boardwalk. Jan Clark was there, waiting, wearing a green silk dress, her hair curled and pinned up.

"Hello, Ruff, I thought you'd come."

"Hello, Jan."

She noticed the big .44 he was wearing, but he kissed her before her puzzlement could form itself into words.

"Now that you're here we can—" she began.

"I don't want you around me tonight, Jan. Not now," he said abruptly.

"But, Ruff . . ." She half-smiled and drew away, cocking her head to study his face. That face was grim and set, and Jan Clark suddenly knew.

"Oh. You know who then?"

"I think I know who killed your father, yes. I mean to find out."

"Here?"

"Here and now. Go over to the hotel, will you? Have a cup of coffee."

"Just leave you, now?"

"That's right. Right now." He held her by her arms until she slowly nodded.

"All right. If you say so, but I'm ordering two cups of coffee. You make sure you show up before yours is cold."

Then, lifting her skirts, she stepped from the board-

177

walk, waited for a gap in the horse and wagon traffic, and crossed the street to Bismarck's hotel.

Ruff turned and started for the hotel door, but he never made it.

Jake Troll appeared from the shadows, putting his bulk in front of Justice. He stroked his red beard and looked Justice up and down.

"Come to play, Justice?" the big man asked.

"Not to play, Troll. Not tonight."

"You got a fancy rig on there," Troll said, nodding at Ruff's presentation revolver. "Me, I'm not wearing one." Troll gingerly opened his coat to show Justice that he had no sidearm. "I don't figure I need one to tear you down. I'm better with my bare hands. Good enough to break your bones from north to south. What do you say, Justice?"

"You thought you needed one the night you came up the hotel alley. You thought you needed two guns, as a matter of fact," Ruff replied.

"That right?" Troll was removing his jacket. A crowd had begun to gather and Troll handed his jacket to his pal, Skitch.

"That's right. You knew you couldn't gun me alone, so you hired a gunny to wait in the stable. I almost believed you that night when you said you'd never seen him before. Especially when you puked your guts out. I'd forgotten how drunk you were, maybe."

"I'm not drunk now, Justice, and now I'm going to kill you. With these." He held up his massive fists and grinned. It was a nasty expression and Justice knew he meant to do it if he could. Ruff was going to give him his try.

Justice took off his coat and folded it, handing it to Joe Carroll. "All these folks want to see you beat up, Justice," Troll said. "You ruined our town for us, cost us all we had. They'll be cheering when you go down to stay."

Justice took off his hat and slowly unbuckled his gun belt. He hadn't got it off before Troll lunged at him, a huge fist hammering down against Ruff's skull.

Justice was slammed back into an upright, his head ringing. Troll, grinning crazily, came in, swinging both fists like a menacing windmill.

An uppercut whipped past Ruff's chin, grazing his nose. A left hand hook was better aimed and it landed against Ruff's ear, sending him staggering down the steps and into the street, where a drunk cowboy riding past hooted derisively. Troll was all over Ruff, throwing a right to the wind, a left to Justice's ribs. Something might have cracked when that one landed, because Justice felt a knifelike pain dig in above his liver.

Ruff backed away, sticking a straight left into Troll's face. The big man barely blinked. A second left didn't have much more impact, but it gave Justice a moment or two to clear his head as Troll backed away a step.

The citizens of Clear Creek lined the boardwalk, and damn them all, they *were* cheering. Cheering for Troll, who moved in with heavy murderous punches, trying to hammer Ruff into the ground.

Ruff still moved away, sticking yet another left into Troll's face. This one brought blood up. A following right nearly missed as Troll backed up a little, but it caught enough skull above the big man's eye to cause Troll to shake his head.

Troll looked toward the boardwalk, where his fellow citizens cheered him on. Then with a grin, he waded in, throwing a barrage of lefts and rights. Ruff caught one on the shoulder, several on his forearms. One snuck in and caught his throat painfully.

Justice countered with a sharp uppercut that

snapped Troll's head back. The big man looked confused as he took a staggering step back. Justice feinted with a left, then gave him the right again. This one stung Ruff's hand, compressing bone against bone sharply. But it didn't sting Justice as badly as it stung Troll. The punch slammed into Troll's jaw and the big man stumbled sideways in a crazy, rubber-legged movement.

Justice didn't let his man off the hook. He came in methodically, throwing crisp, sharp punches. Each one stilled some of the cheering from the boardwalk. Each one hammered Troll until he had his back against a horse at the hitch rail. The big man could go no farther, he tried to fight back, but he had had it. His eyes were glazed over. He held those meaty fists up protectively, trying to fend off Justice, unable to strike back with his own blows.

Ruff went to the body, once, twice, and the big hands dropped. Justice needed one more good punch and he threw it now. An overhand right hooked over Troll's lowered defenses and landed solidly on the hinge of his jaw.

Troll's eyes rolled back and his lights went out. He sat down in the mud beneath the horse. Ruff walked to Joe Carroll and retrieved his gear, looking into the eyes of the people of Clear Creek.

"Maybe," he told them, "that town of yours deserved to die."

Troll was stirring beneath the horse now and Justice went back there, yanking him to his feet. "You hired that gunny, didn't you?"

Troll panted. "Yes." Blood trickled from his puffed lips. He tried to pull away from Justice, but Justice jerked him back savagely.

"You paid him with a gold coin. Where did you get that coin, Troll?"

180

"From"—Troll's hand lifted feebly—"Luke Stansford. He owed me money. Asked me would I take the gold piece."

Ruff's hand opened and Troll half-fell, holding his head with one hand as he leaned against the horse. Ruff turned on Stansford, his hand lowering toward the big presentation Colt. People shifted away from the teamster, who stood with his hand near his own holstered pistol.

"Where did you get the gold, Stansford?" Justice demanded.

"You guess, scout," Luke Stansford replied. There was no give in the man, it seemed.

"My guess is you got it from Clive Hickam. My guess is you killed the man. Why, I'm not sure. Maybe you thought you knew enough to find the rest of the gold without him. But I think you killed him. Took that twisted arrow from the burial site and ran it into his back."

"Keep on guessing, then," Stansford said.

"You did it?" Ruff asked.

"Sure. I did it," Stansford said. "I wanted his gold."

"Stop it," May Stansford shrieked. "Stop lying! You and your ridiculous man's pride."

May Stansford looked older, shaken, and gray as she stepped out on the plankwalk. "He didn't kill Clive Hickam." She touched her breast. "I did it! I did it because I loved him and he didn't love me. He gave me that gold piece and the arrow. That was all he gave me. He never gave me love. But I loved him and this big stupid lout here knew it. He had culture, brains, did Clive Hickam, something my husband didn't even understand."

"Stop it, May," Stansford said quietly. "I said I killed Hickam, didn't I, Justice?"

May Stansford laughed crazily. "See—he'd rather

181

hang or get himself shot than admit that his wife was with another man. A man who could only talk about other women. That's why Clear Creek hated him. He was always after someone. I hated Clive in the end. He always talked about Jan Clark, how clever she was. I hated her before I ever met her."

"She's his daughter, Mrs. Stansford. Clive Hickam's daughter," Ruff Justice said.

The woman paused for a minute, letting that sink in. Then she shrugged it away. "It doesn't matter. Nothing matters. Clive Hickam loved me. He took me to bed, he made love to me, and then he told me what a foolish woman I was. Of course I killed him. Of course I did! And do you know what kind of a lover he was compared to this—this so-called man here?"

Luke Stansford moved before anyone could stop him. His Colt came up and he shot his wife through the breast. He must have known it was suicide, but he switched his sights to Justice and tried to fire again.

The big silver-mounted Colt was already in Ruff's hand, though, already blazing away, and Stansford took three bullets, each of which turned him until he slammed into the plank wall of the town hall and folded up to lie in a pool of his own blood.

Ruff holstered the Colt, snapping the spring hinge back into place. He looked at the two dead people, at the citizens of Clear Creek, at Jake Troll, who still stood next to the horse, Jenny Farnsworth in his arms. Then he turned sharply and walked away.

Bismarck had a good marshal who could straighten things out from here on. Justice had a cold cup of coffee and a good warm woman waiting for him.

WESTWARD HO!

The follwing is the opening section from the next novel in the gun-blazing, action-packed new Ruff Justice series from Signet:

RUFF JUSTICE #27:
THE THUNDER RIDERS

1

She had a gun but she wasn't quite ready to use it. The tall man in buckskins was just stepping out of his trousers, crossing the room toward the bed, his silhouette lean and masculine, in the light of the low-burning lantern on the hotel table.

Outside, Bismarck, Dakota Territory, continued its night of drinking and gambling, carousing and violence. Inside, the bed was soft and warm, the sheets forming themselves around the contours of the blond woman's lush body.

The senator's daughter looked up at the tall man who stood beside the bed, naked and hard. His hair was long and dark, brushed down across his scarred shoulders; his mouth curved wickedly beneath his drooping black mustache.

Ada Sinclair reached out and let her hand grope upward from the tall man's thigh to his erect manhood.

"What are you waiting for?" she asked. She scooted to the far side of the bed, feeling the hard bulge of the Colt revolver beneath her pillow. The revolver she would use to stop the tall man's heart.

Later.

Later, after he had finished climbing on her, kissing her throat and breasts and thighs, her soft, flat abdomen, her hungry full lips. It seemed a shame, but they said it had to be done. What a waste of manhood.

Ruff Justice was his name, and he was built long and lean and angular, with ropy muscles, a solid stomach, hard-muscled thighs. He was a scout and a frontiersman, a hunter and a lover of women—he knew all of his crafts well.

The senator's daughter lifted the sheet and Ruff Justice crawled in beside her to place his naked, needful body next to hers, to let his callused hands run across her breasts, teasing the taut pink nipples, dropping to her slender, sleek thighs.

Ada's breath began to come rapidly. She lay dreamily against the pillow, arm thrown limply to one side, waves of long golden hair fanned out against the pillowcase. Her eyes were half-closed, lips half-parted as the tall man methodically worked his way over her body with probing fingers and hungry mouth.

The senator had come west a few months back to look into the situation on the plains. Back East, some were still crying for the army to avenge Little Big Horn, others screaming that the plains tribes had had enough, that they ought to be offered an honorable peace and the United States ought to stick by it.

184

Excerpt from THE THUNDER RIDERS

On the plains of Dakota, too, there were a lot of people who had been hurt by the Sioux and the Cheyenne and were now demanding that every last "wild" Indian be buried beneath the prairie, while others thought that the war would never end unless a just treaty was signed.

Rather than listen to speech makers, headline writers, and the often incoherent letters of his constituents, Senator Cotton Sinclair had done what few others were willing to do: he had gotten up from his desk, stepped on a train, and come out to see for himself what in hell was happening.

As a bonus, he had brought his daughter west, and Ada Sinclair was justification enough for the senator's existence. She was sleek, cultured, beautiful beyond the dreams of most plainsmen, full-breasted, and so slender at the waist that Justice could place his hands around her there. Blessed with firm, flaring hips that swayed hypnotically when she walked, she didn't draw the usual collection of jeers, whistles, remarks, and catcalls when she strolled through Bismarck twirling her parasol. The men just stood and stared in sheer disbelief.

If she was something dressed, on the street, she was much more in bed: hungry for love, sleek and compelling, her kisses practiced and eager, her body a dream meant to comfort a needful man.

She lifted her hands now and her fingers ran lightly over Justice's hard buttocks, drawing him nearer to her before she lifted and spread her knees with a sigh, offering him the sanctuary of her warm, tender body.

"I didn't thank you for showing me Bismarck," Ada Sinclair said. Her fingers had wrapped around Ruff's shaft and now she gently guided him in, teasing him.

"Orders," Justice said. "Your father has some pull with the colonel, you know."

"Is this orders?" she asked, arching her back, holding his hand to her full breast, smiling up out of the depths of her pleasure as Justice penetrated another fraction of an inch.

"Sure, that's the only time I'd ever do something like this," Ruff Justice said. He kissed her neck beneath her ear, smelling the faint, haunting scent of her perfume.

"Orders," she said from far away. Her hands wrapped around his neck and she clung to him, pressing her body against his, her pelvis striking out hungrily. "Here's an order—deeper, Ruff, give it to me. Fix it for me."

Breathed into his ear, the order was an easy one to follow. Justice fell into a tangle of love with the blonde, rolling from side to side, arms and legs clutching, mouths clinging to flesh. Justice's rhythm, deep and insistent, brought cries of joy from the lips of the senator's daughter until with a last, nearly anguished gasp she reached a solid, trembling climax.

"God, that's why I came west, that's why . . ."

Justice still swayed against her, tasting her breasts, her sweet full lips. She stroked his long dark hair, looking up at him with pleasure and a sort of feminine pride from the depths of her emerald-green eyes.

She felt him tense, sway against her, felt his body thrust against her one final time before he found his release, rolling her onto her back to hover over her and look down at her, arms braced, eyes searching.

"What would your commanding officer say?" Ada asked, her finger tracing a pattern across Justice's solid chest.

"What would your father say?" Justice asked, bending low to kiss those full, warm lips again.

"My father wouldn't say anything. He'd simply have you shot," Ada Sinclair answered.

"Would he, now? You come from a violent family."

"Yes, we . . ." But the smile faded from her lips and from her eyes.

Justice wondered what deep nerve he had touched with the remark. He lowered himself again to lie beside her, feeling her occasional tight embrace, the searching of her hands, the light kiss that came from time to time as he began to doze into a satisfied sleep.

Ada Sinclair sighed, let her finger run along the tall man's eyebrow toward his ear. Then she kissed her finger and touched it to that ear.

It was a shame, she thought, such a goddamn shame. She looked at the moon peering in through the window of their ground-floor hotel room, watching its dull sheen for a time. Then she removed her left hand from Ruff's shoulder, alert for any sign that the man wasn't asleep.

Her hand went under her pillow and her fingers touched the smooth walnut grip of the big Colt revolver there, slowly wrapping around it.

Ada glanced again at the window and at the one opposite. Beside that window sat a chair with her clothes on it. It was there that Justice had seated her and had slowly begun undressing her: unbuttoning her shoes, removing her stockings, each step followed by a kiss—on her calf, her thigh as he worked his way upward, on her shoulders and breasts as he undid her dress and slid it from her.

There was a man who knew how to make love. He acted as if he had no place else to go, nothing else on his mind. That the world had begun and ended in this room with this act. It was truly a shame to have to kill Ruff Justice.

Ada lifted her thigh from Justice's carefully, watching his nose twitch once, his fingers clench. Then she was away from him, out of the bed, standing naked over the army scout, the huge Peacemaker in her hands, cocked and ready to fire.

"Good-bye, Ruff Justice," the senator's daughter said under her breath. "Sorry."

The glass in the window before her was smashed out by a rifle barrel and Ada Sinclair shifted her aim, jerking the gun upward as she yanked too hard on the trigger. The bullet flew into the wall, scattering plaster everywhere. From the window an answering bullet was fired, narrowly missing Ada's head.

Ruff Justice had rolled from the bed, reaching automatically for his holstered pistol, which he had hung on a bedside chair, but the pistol was gone.

He saw Ada Sinclair, naked, gun in hand, ducking low as she moved across the hotel room toward the opposite window.

"Ada!" Justice called out, and as he did, the woman swung the muzzle of her pistol toward him. Justice ducked below the bed as the Colt revolver spat flame and a .44 slug ripped its way through mattress and bed frame, leaving the bedding smoldering.

Then Ada was at the window, stepping over the sill as she grabbed for the dress she had left behind, sending another wild shot toward the window opposite.

Plaster flew and the gun's report echoed through the room. A cloud of black powder smoke hung over the bed. Ada was gone. The window curtains moved lightly in the evening breeze and Justice heard several light footsteps as the senator's daughter made her escape up the alley.

Puzzled and angry, Justice rose and walked to the far window. The breeze was cool against his naked body. He found his empty holster under Ada Sinclair's petticoats, but his pistol was nowhere to be seen. Presumably it was his own gun that the woman had fired at him.

"Why?" Justice asked himself. It made no sense at all. Ada Sinclair had come to town, a visiting dignitary, allowed herself to be taken to Justice's bed, and apparently enjoyed what had followed.

"Maybe you've lost your touch," Justice muttered. He slammed the window shut and turned. As he did, the woman with the dark hair and Indian eyes came in through the other window.

She had a Winchester repeater in her hands and wore her hair tied back with a piece of rawhide string. She had on a white blouse, leather vest, and leather divided skirt. A length of golden leg showed itself as she stepped over the sill.

Ada Sinclair had worn corset, petticoats, chemise, and pantaloons under her clothing. It had taken Justice a long while to get them all off.

This one wore nothing beneath her blouse. Dark-nippled breasts jutted against the white fabric so clearly that she might as well have worn nothing. Her legs were long, her mouth sensual yet firm.

She carried the Winchester low, the muzzle pointed at Ruff's belly.

"You have the right room, lady?" Justice asked. He stood naked, one hand on the wall, eyeing her closely.

She looked around the hotel room cautiously, coming forward another stride. "You are Ruff Justice?" she asked. There was an accent to her voice and Justice knew then what she was. He had heard Cheyenne Indians speak before.

"That's right," he replied.

"Army scout. Man of legends."

Ruff smiled. "Army scout."

"Man of legends?" the Indian woman insisted.

"Maybe. Have you come to kill me, Cheyenne woman?" he asked in her own tongue.

"Not you," she answered in English. "Not to kill you, but now that I am here, I want to know." Her eyes roamed over his body, pausing with interest at his crotch. "I want to see if you are the man the legends say."

Then she opened her blouse with one hand, nearly popping the buttons as her honey-colored breasts bobbed free of their thin covering.

"Show me now, man of legend, or I will have to shoot you."

...saying softly, "Here it is." ... sound. There was an armed lookout above and below ... knew then what the wolf ... had faced ... Indians ... on horses ...

⊘ SIGNET BOOKS

HOLD ON TO YOUR SADDLE!

(0451)

☐ SKINNER, by F.M. Parker. (138139—$2.75)
☐ THE GREAT GUNFIGHTERS OF THE WEST, by C. Breihan. (111206—$2.25)
☐ LUKE SUTTON: OUTRIDER, by Leo P. Kelley. (134869—$2.50)
☐ THE ARROGANT GUNS, by Lewis B. Patten. (138643—$2.75)
☐ GUNS AT GRAY BUTTE, by Lewis B. Patten. (135741—$2.50)
☐ LAWMAN'S CHOICE by Ray Hogan (112164—$1.95)
☐ PILGRIM by Ray Hogan (095766—$1.75)
☐ CORUNDA'S GUNS, by Ray Hogan. (133382—$2.50)
☐ APACHE MOUNTAIN JUSTICE, by Ray Hogan. (137760—$2.75)
☐ THE DOOMSDAY CANYON, by Ray Hogan. (139216—$2.75)

Prices slightly higher in Canada

Buy them at your local
bookstore or use coupon
on next page for ordering.

THE OLD WILD WEST

(0451)

- [ ] THE LAST CHANCE by Frank O'Rourke (115643—$1.95)
- [ ] SEGUNDO by Frank O'Rourke (117816—$2.25)
- [ ] VIOLENCE AT SUNDOWN by Frank O'Rourke (111346—$1.95)
- [ ] COLD RIVER by William Judson (137183—$2.75)
- [ ] TOWN TAMER by Frank Gruber (110838—$1.95)
- [ ] SIGNET DOUBLE WESTERN: BLOOD JUSTICE & THE VALIANT BUGLES by Gordon D. Shireffs (133390—$3.50)
- [ ] SIGNET DOUBLE WESTERN: BITTER SAGE & THE BUSHWACKERS by Frank Gruber (129202—$3.50)
- [ ] SIGNET DOUBLE WESTERN: QUANTRELL'S RAIDERS & TOWN TAMER by Frank Gruber (127773—$3.50)
- [ ] SIGNET DOUBLE WESTERN: COMANCHE' & RIDE THE WILD TRAIL by Cliff Farrell (115651—$2.50)
- [ ] SIGNET DOUBLE WESTERN: CROSS FIRE & THE RENEGADE by Cliff Farrell (123891—$2.95)
- [ ] SIGNET DOUBLE WESTERN: TROUBLE IN TOMBSTONE & BRAND OF A MAN by Tom Hopkins and Thomas Thompson (116003—$2.50)

Prices slightly higher in Canada

Buy them at your local bookstore or use this convenient coupon for ordering.

NEW AMERICAN LIBRARY,
P.O. Box 999, Bergenfield, New Jersey 07621

Please send me the books I have checked above. I am enclosing $_____
(please add $1.00 to this order to cover postage and handling). Send check
or money order—no cash or C.O.D.'s. Prices and numbers are subject to change
without notice.

Name_____

Address_____

City_____State_____Zip Code_____
Allow 4-6 weeks for delivery.
This offer is subject to withdrawal without notice.